AF508966

May I Be Your Better Half

Mahesh R Abishek

SATR.CO.IN

Published by Satr, 2017

ISBN-13: 9788193409343

ISBN-10: 8193409345

Price: ₹

Satr, a self-publishing imprint of Woven Words Publishers, Vill: Raipur, P.O: Raipur Paschimbar, Dist: Purba Midnapore, Pin: 721401, West Bengal, India.
satr.co.in

Printed and bound in India

To all the love puppies of our Nation,

To the best feel in the planet, LOVE,

To the land of Respect, Paddy and Protection (Tirunelveli),

To my dear parents, brother and our dear pet 'LEO',

To the real incidents, which are the reasons of this book.

For the girl I admired, who impressed me much like no one in this world.

ACKNOWLEDGEMENTS

I am out of words to thank you dear readers, friends, bookish guy/girl like me for picking up "May I Be your Better Half?"

I want to take this opportunity to thank each and every person, who patted on my shoulder and encouraged me a lot to make this possible.

Thanks Dad, Mom and my brother Mahesh Aravind for being my never ending support, especially dad who is my ATM still, from my formative years. Loads and loads of thanks to you all.

My sincere thanks to my publisher SATR Publishers, Mosiur Rehman (Head of SATR Publishers) and his editing team for bringing this book wonderful. I personally thank Nita Samantaray (Author) for providing me this platform of publishing idea. And I have to thank you my dears here:

Ebenezer, Ignesh, Alwar – Thanks for knowing that I can write and encouraged me a lot through many of the things even though you people are distant apart from me.

Prabhavathy G – My sweetest sissy, who really concerned a lot on my writings and gave me the idea to proceed my scribbled writings into a gorgeous book. Without her words and motivations, this writing could have been stopped in that old three small pages itself.

Tamilamuthan, Dharma, Suganya, Shaiqa, Revathi, Kamatchi – My extended family like friends who supported my even it was with flaws. They have a great part of correcting the mistakes I did while writing. They never stopped being my side.

Sujeetha & Sandhya – I am very happy to mention the editors of my side, who got my first manuscript landed in their hands. You people are more than a precious editor, you' re my awesome buddies.

Santhosh & Sriram – My stupidest and loveliest mates, who created publicity always for me in real world and virtual social networks. I have to say, even I feared that whether am writing a love story or a bad one by their critics. Their strong support is always a ladder for me.

Adheep, Irfan, Laxman, Sarita, Sethukkarasi – My wonderful friends, who always read my writings and showed enthusiasm in giving me the best thoughts they have all the time.

Balaji, Vijayalakshmi R – They lovely treasure of me who immediately read my fb writings posts, poems and giving me the review even at their busy timings.

Ashi Kalim, Author – Who helped me to make my English good and better. Her help during her busiest times was very precious and much adorable.

Vignesh, Sairam and Venkatesh V – The lovely idiots who tolerated my midnight writings with lights on calmly, even though it killed their sleep many nights. Not only my roommates and friends, they are always a part of me.

Thanks to my dear friends Jasphin, Sindhuja, Sibi, Arun Sundar, Vijay Sankar, Prazad, Udhay Kumar, VijayBaskar, Manigandan, Sruthi, Preeti Kamak who supported me in my every part of writing.

I love to thank the 'Madras Techies' Fb page admins and the followers who posted and gave comments of my writings. My hearty thanks to all the Solartians and the people of my TamilNadu.

Tremendous thanks to you 'Deepthi'. Without you this is just a pile of blank papers.

And finally, I thank you all for being the part of this book directly or indirectly. Always with love towards you all.

MAHESH R ABISHEK

The Pain in my Heart

I was longing to see her,

I was longing to get closer to her,

Time was not to wait like me,

It went by its own rules,

I was trying to be a man,

To carry over my responsibilities,

And finally, the day came when I confessed
to her,

I thought things would be in my favour,

But seemed that God had other ideas,

She is someone else's soul mate now,

She was married,

While I was trying to be in a position,

To carry over my responsibilities,

There ended my Love Story!!

-   What I never forgot was... her
    Smile.

Always with the memories of your
    smile ☺

PROLOGUE

She could hear her watch ticking. It was not her fault to be in that empty road at that time. She didn't deserve it too. All of a sudden it had happened. Mild wind whispered the lunatic fear inside her. As a girl, she shouldn't be alone in an Indian society at late nights. Despite of showing her fear, she pretended to be brave and started walking.

Braveness is like a cloth on a thorn, it may be torn easily, until if a slight pressure of fear rule over it. Better she might have stayed where she was two hours before. If she was like that, it wasn't her. Never in her dreams, she had thought that could have happened. Even she was a firm believer of god, no God of any religion or none have saved a girl in her bad times as we have seen and known.

Fear drove in her mind, as she started feeling weak. Her footsteps went on its pace towards the single silent road. In another three minutes, she heard the engine sound of a bike. She tilted her head and looked on her backside.

A man looked like a native guy got down from his Yamaha bike and walked towards her. She opened her mouth to let her words out. Before she could have spoken, he came was looking into her eyes and she stood shocked.

"Seven thousand rupees, final rate for the night. I have a safe place and I have rubbers for protection," he said with a sly smile.

No reply came from her. She was in an absolute state where the heart and brain stops working. Started sweating on her face. People can talk about women empowerment, welfare and rights. But this whole society is a shit, which have all the shit eaters in this planet.

"Hello, don't worry. I won't be so rude and you can have my contact. Looks like you are a fresher and you are scared," he uttered casually.

She knew this won't get over until she clears him out. "I came here mistakenly by the wrong direction shown in my GPS". She replied calmly. He was in no mood to hear her words and all. Her beauty and her situation of being alone gave some more confidence to him.

"C'mon. Don't act like a virgin. You must have tasted a few. Add me in that list now." He said with a strong tone.

Pain is not the one which tears your physical strength, it is the knife that puts a nice deep cut over your heart and makes you to lose all your mental strength and fuck your brains out.

It was the state which every female in this society faces, where no baby girl, girl child, girl, woman, mom, even a granny can walk in the road alone. They will get raped, abused or they'll be called to give pleasure for the filthy lusty meat of some human-animal's sex thirst.

People can discuss in talk shows, talk about the flaws in the society, but no one have the courage and intention to pluck the weeds India is growing. On the other hand, some politicians say the dressing style of the woman receives the brutality on them. Some religious saints and preachers say, the bad luck of the girl's and the God will show mercy on her in heaven.

She headed south. He followed her. She broke into tears and couldn't turn back and was helpless. Within a fraction of second, she felt a strong hold of a man's palm on her shoulder.

'Sight'O Pedia

Clouds brushed the pale orange sun which was about to set. Abhinav leant his back on the boat, parked in the beach sands. His legs were on theshore, where the ocean tides kissed his feet with slowly. Both his eyes were focused on the sun, which was about to set in another fifteen minutes of the Indian Standard Time.

On the left of him, the shoreline met the famous atomic power station in nearly twenty kilometers. And on the right of him, it meets the tip of the India… 'The Cape of Capricorn.'

He was at the 'Rastha Kaadu' Beach sands, which gave the absolute sight of that two above. Apart from that, there was a complete silence except the sounds of the tides. It must be a pleasant evening. But it was not.

When pain grew every second inside the heart, soul started to turn weak. Experiencing that, he was in no mood to enjoy the beautiful natural view before his sight. None was there except the reptiles in the beach. The breeze touched him, whispered a name in his ears. That was the name he inhaled and exhaled for years - *"Deepthi."*

Abhinav felt saw a girl coming towards him. It was Achu. She was digesting the pain he was undergoing. Achu looked in his eyes and held his wrist with her hand. She dragged him to leave for home. All she needed was him to not be in that state. The hardest state one shouldn't be in. They walked through the road and got into Achu's Swift D'zire. She drove it to "Bang's Eatout." Achu is his colleague, a well-wisher and a good friend of Abhinav.

Being crazy, she had always been a crowd gathering girl, who entertains her friend-circle a lot. She was a girl in her early twenties having an unstoppable passion to make everyone happy all the time. Achu had a great fond of bikes especially in KTM Duke Ranges. She was also a party lover, who says no to alcohol, but dumps all the mocktails of the world into her stomach. She was approached by many but no guy war successful. Being in the metropolitan city she loves to be fashionable and also balance her traditional look.

'I thought you were at your home, and never thought, you will be here' said Achu in a disappointed tone.

'I don't want my parents to see me suffer. I try to hide all these, still am failing. Achu and I couldn't control ourself.' A single drop of tear came out from his left eye. When a person cries and the first drop of tears comes from the right eye, it's because of happiness, butif it's from the left, it's pain. Achu ordered two pilipili chicken leg fries and two blue mojitos.

Abhinav was still silent. But Achu knew how to break his silence and make him smile. "Am hungry pa, how long will they take to prepare two pilipili? Are you going to speak or not? Please don't keep your face like that Abhinav, I can't see that. Ok come on tell me about your love."

The word "love," especially "your love" brought a smile on his face. "Habbbaa finally you smiled. That's my Abhinav. 'The only reason why I loved Monday mornings more than Friday evenings….

2 Aug 2007 [Thursday]

Palayamkottai, Tirunelveli

"Dude, it's almost 8am. We are already late. See, I am not in mood to ruin my day getting torn up by the Rockfeeder Vincent," Dev made his point sharply.

"Relax machan, you can't never choose anything when it comes in the terms on taste. Already I am driving crazy with the hunger of this early morning. Let's get some vadas and we'll reach the tuition in less than fifteen minutes," said Abhinav.

They were at the Jayanthi Tea shop, which is famous for their hot vadas and spicy tea. Vadas are still one rupee each and it turned to be the daily snack of thousands of people in Palayamkottai, Tirunelveli. Dev and Abhinav parked their Hero cycles in the neem shade near the Tea stall and started having vadas. With the delicious Red chutney, it tasted well and they had five each.

"I told you right, we are almost ten minutes late. Ready to get scold by him."

"Don't worry dude, it won't be our day if we aren't worshipped with his words," Abhinav told casually.

They stepped inside the door of their Math coaching center. Mr. Vincent was teaching the Integral Calculus with great zeal. As they made themselves inside there, he came furiously and threw them out of the class.

"Shit. He is such a moron man. How can he balance his feelings as he always barks like a dumb bitchy dog?" Dev said, with a dull gaze.

"Everything happens for good man. Think positive. The idiot is here inside and the world is outside. And you know what I mean to say!!" Abhinav delivered his naughty statement with a pulpy smile.

"Yep Abhinav. You are such a guy who always matches my mind with your taste."

They were at the opposite of the Rose Mary Matriculation School. Abhinav brought two cans of coke for him and Dev.

"Man, that girl Varsha is so beautiful. Her boyfriend Karan is so lucky yaar," Dev dropped his jaw on seeing her.

"Uff… Bitch Please, don't let your saliva out for other guy's girl yaar. It could be only one you should die for. Others are just your soups" Abhinav kidded him with a smile.

"You can Abhinav, being seventeen, you know all the tactics to work on a girl to make her flatten. But still you are apart from us in what we are doing. You come to sight girls, But, you don't stalk. What comes to your mind when the term 'girl' comes?" Dev asked curiously to know what he had in his mind

"Saints calledthem the flowers of the worlds. Kings called them the Angels of this planet. But women are butterflies dude, they become precious and beautiful day by day. You can stare, stalk, impress, imagine, dream them. But you can't never get into their heart, unless they drive you inside them" Abhinav made his sentence firmly.

Abhinav dropped his pock-can without his brain's acknowledgement when he saw her. The girl was in her White salwar with brown sheeted notes in her hand. She was walking happily in the middle of the street with her little feet and her own shadow was accompanying her. Having 5'4" in height, she was a perfect looking girl a man chooses to marry.

Combed her hair in the traditional style, as her center line of the head vertically separated the sides of her hair. Her forehead had a little line of saffron indicated her love of god. She let her hair combed greatly and hung it down to her spine. Her charming smile over her sweet strawberry coloured lips had won his senses. He stood there still as she crossed him. She raised her head up, and gave a quick look on his eyes.

He was no more in this Earth, he felt his legs weren't pulled by gravity and was at air. Abhinav was poisoned slowly by her 11.8 seconds of presence. The cheeks of her were absolutely beautiful, which completely remembered him of rasgullas.

She was visibly cute and not in his dreams he had thought about getting a chance to see a girl like her. "Man, how could she be like this! I wish I could believe in God somehow." He giggled inside in a desperate thought.

Men are always men in what they do. A thin gold chain on her neck drove him crazy to just look on it for hours. The rays of the sun fell on her pale pinkish skin and gave a golden electroplated tone. She was completely awesome in her looks and he dared to even walk behind her. In fact, he was entirely stuck with his body parts malfunctioning by just a sight of a pretty girl in the town.

The word 'Crush' hit his mind for a minute and she went inside her campus. He blushed right in front of Dev, who gave a nasty look on him.

A smile came over his lips and the enthusiasm of seeing her the next time ruled Abhinav's mind out. He remembered the second their eyes met.

Leant towards them,

Looked curiously at them,

Loved the feel it gave,

Lost myself in them,

Rolled my thoughts in my dreams,

Rotted my innocence like a freak,

Ran towards that ravishing honey,

Resized my brain in my own head,

Are they magnetic???

Asked my mind,

Are they my love wine???

Asked my beats,

No words to express,

Nothing can match them,

No one can compare,

None can be born

They are pure,

They are lovely,

They are lustful,

They are the sweet gaze,

Those are her's,

Little grapes,

Dipped in the ice-creams,

Intruded inside me,

Gravity has no role, when it is in this planet.

Her eyes…. The eyes which had wounded me a minute ago.

It had been three weeks since he saw her. All of a sudden, he fell for her, like a teetotaler addicts to marijuana. One side look of a girl is more vulnerable than an addiction to alcohol.

"Many rehabilitation centers are there to pull us out of the alcoholic addiction, but none existed in this planet to take a man out of the sweetness he tasted from a girl's look and her exotic smile. One should know to tackle it, else life will be a great blunder" Abhinav thought in his mind.

"Better you must have a camera phone dude. In this past six months, you might have clicked a pic of her right, so you don't have to worry about not seeing her on these days," Dev said with a sad tone.

"It's not about just an image of her dude. I admire her. More than her beauty something pulls me towards her. The thing is, our classmates may talk about this as just a fatal attraction if they came to know but sooner or later I might break it." Abhinav told Dev and he replied with a "Ooh."

However, Abhinav had a crush on her just by her looks, He felt that she was the girl for him. It might be an instinct or over confidence, but over confidence is somewhat better than the zero confidence.

R.I.P Movies – I am a Book-Lover

George University,

Chennai

"You're such a dumb head, Deepthi. Come and join with us. Throw that book out and see this hunk dear," Sumi said in an anxious tone. "What if I get a date with him? He's so hot. How can a girl dump a guy like him just for a small lie?" he murmured in a disappointed tone. She was watching a Hindi serial in the last row of the class with her mobile kept with the support of the first bench to give a good view to watch.

Deepthi was reading the newly arrived 'Two States' by Chetan Bhagat. "Try to get out of that. Guys are dying to talk with you. You have surprisingly become the most beautiful girl in this college without publicity. Don't be a book worm!" Sumi said with jealousy.

"Correct it. Am not a book worm, am a book lover," Deepthi replied with a smile. Her dimples over her lovely cheekbones looked with no flaw in her cheeks beauty.

"Ok Ms.Book lover, you can't find a prince for you in books. You better go for a date darling."

"I am not saying am not interested in that but still, I don't feel the need now," Deepthi replied with a wink.

"Don't talk like shit Deepthi. You sound like Kamal Hassan's movie dialogues," Sumi giggled.

The class was over and the break time had started. They started walking towards the canteen. A guy with white crisp shirt and blue denims called Sumi by her name. She just turned her head to 120 degrees and looked at him. 'Sumi, I need to talk with you.

You are in my dreams and in my thoughts. Day by day you are killing me.' Sumi shrugged and he continued.

"I don't think you are the prettiest one alive, but you are the pretty one in my eyes. I can go up to any extent to hold you in my arms." He told with a passionate look in his eyes. She didn't know what to say. She simply pulled Deepthi and continued walking. He followed them and begged Sumi to respond.

That was the bad idea. When he started begging, Sumi turned and showed her middle finger to him. On her perception, a man should have some attitude, and not behave like a shoe licking dog.

"So, it was a flash proposal yaar. Whole college saw that and you, Sumi, are you a hell? You scattered that little guy's heart dude," Abhinav mocked Sumi with a naughty smile.

Abhinav was doing his third year of ComputerScience and Engineering with Sumi and Deepthi. He was their bestie from the starting of the second year. At first, he was so close only with Deepthi. Later, he developed his friendship with Sumi too. Even the two talked about the new scandals of the Bollywood casually, while Deepthi shut her earsalways and got annoyed.

"Girls, I have planned to visit the 'BheemRao Orphanage' this Saturday. Almost 800 children are living there. And they are in need of good clothes and food. I have already talked with 'Mr. Pankaj Shetty [C.E.O of Pankaj Granites India Ltd.]' He assured me that he can offer me a fund of 3 lakh rupees and I have already saved some of my pocket money and the extra bucks we got by the sponsors of the symposium we conducted last month. Are you girls in?" Abhinav said and took a sip of his Kesar milkshake.

"No yaar. I already have plans. Rajveer is coming home this Saturday after a longtime. I have to be there." Sumi told. Rajveer was her younger brother who was doing a scholarship research about Stem cells at the Germany Institute of Science and Research, Berlin.

"Ok. You carry on. Deepthi?"

"Do u have to ask me for that. Am already in before you say that." She told with a brisk tone. And they started to their classes after their drinks were finished.

"Aparna, your hair smells so good baby. If my nose guessed it correct, its lavender flavored hair spray, right?" John leaned towards Aparna's hair from the back desk he sat and asked.

She kept silent as she knew he was always of that kind. He used to flirt with everyone, but never got into a relationship. He dated many girls, but he never broke their hearts.

In spite of making them fall in love, he always had fallen for enjoyment only. John was a well built, clean shaved, six packed man with his own limits and controls.

Abhinav gave a mock punch on her head and made him to sit on the seat as Professor Chandru came in.

"Babe, I just faint when that rosy lip gloss on your sweet lips hit my eyes. It is inviting me to taste it. Come on, my tongue deserves it." He told in a seductive tone, without knowing all the eyes in the class were on him including Chandru's. John skipped a beat.

Chandru came near to him. "If you are hot, don't flirt or watch porn and masturbate. Find a friend with benefits and do all the stuff, until you bore on that for the week. Even after that you like the girl, then flirt and make her as your companion. Because spending useless nights with just being hot is like licking the outer core of the groundnut without tasting the inner part of it."

He cleared his statement and went. John was speechless, when Abhinav almost fell on the ground by his uncontrollable ROFL.

Normal friends are the ones who help you a lot, who loves you a lot. But they never can be a bestie. Best friends are those who yell at you like 'You die moron,' when you fall sick but give you the blood from his/her own body to you.

They'll put a VR Gear on your eyes and make you to watch Real Madrid vs Barcelona when, you are not able to get up from your bed. That kind of one is John for Abhinav and Sumi for Deepthi.

John and Abhinav came out of the class and seated on the concrete bench out of their class. As they were talking about the Sunday's plan, a girl came from the opposite block towards them. Abhinav didn't mind her, but John had his time. His mouth was wide open and he smiled like the cow from HappyDent advertisement by showing all his teeth out.

She stood in front of Abhinav with her hands crossed and looked directly on his eyes. He looked so gentle. Every girl deserves a caring guy like him. According to him *making love with our loved one or sleeping with her with our hands hugged is nothing special than taking care of our soul mate during her pregnancy and being supportive for her at her periods.*

As she was standing infront of him, she never skipped a second from looking at him directly. Abhinav kept calm and waited for her to start. She just came near him and touched his hair gently and rubbed her right palm over it. Abhinav shrugged and moved her hand from his head.

"I have a huggggggeeeeeee crush on you. I am not saying you should be mine. I know you don't know me too. The girls in this college are being likesheep in crowd and looking, longing and dreaming about you, I want to be the admirer, soul owner, and the partner in your love crimes," she continued.

"I am not here to say "Love you." I just came over here to say I must be a good match if you choose me. By the way, am Priyanka from 2nd year ECE department," She added and John dropped his jaw.

"Seriously dude. You have a mole right in the middle of your chest. Without running behind the girls, you just drive them to you with no hardness!" He expressed his words out in a loud manner.

Sumi came there at correct time. "So, here is the guy, who don't need any dating sites to grab a date, people. Take a bow champ" She grinned. Abhinav left the place letting them to laugh for a while.

A Twin Monster Ride

Wonder La,

Bangalore

Abhinav, Deepthi, Sumi and John were at Bangalore for their Industrial Visit. After three boring days at industries, IT companies lectures and travel they finally got a place to rock on and enjoy.

"Yummy, tastes like a real mango's pulp," Sumi loved the taste and sweetness of the Mango ice-cream she had.

"Girls, are you up for the Water games? There is a long water tunnel at the top of that floor which takes a ride to ground floor. Just try it," John gave a suggestion.

"Are you kidding? Just erase that thing from your mind. We are going to take adventurous rides. Columbus, Break dance followed up by Twin Monster."

John started sweating almost when her heard all these. He was really not into these adventurous games. He could be in water rides for a day, but he couldn't go for just a ride mentioned above by Sumi.

"Let's go boys. It should be fun. Chalo Deepthi. You have the Camera right. We'll click selfies when we ride that horse," She pointed Twin Monster.

Twin Monster hadtwo seats per side like it has eight sides. It rotated for 480 degrees and also went up and down in the meantime. Abhinav was very casual about this where Deepthi was also uncomfortable with this machine. Sumi and Deepthi seated adjacently. John and Abhinav was at their opposite sides. They were locked by a shoulder strap and seat belts for their protection.

"And the ride starts now. Bang Bang Bang'oh" Sumi shouted in the air.

John howled a lot. He was almost started crying. "Let me go you monkeys. Am not into this," he yelled. In order to reduce the fear, he closed his eyes. It was a bad idea. Due to the spin movement of the machine, he started to panic.

Sumi knew it was the time to drag John into some childish fun. She already had some nut bolts in her pockets when they started to Wonder La from their rooms. She shouted for his name.

He opened his eyes slowly. All the three saw the entire fear and panic inside his head. She tapped on his shoulders and asked,

"Are these from your seat??"

John froze at the moment she showed the nut bolts to him. He saw that with his own eyes and he just imagined how long he would fly if he lost his ass from the seat on that rotations.

"Stop it Stop it !!! I am going to be thrown out. Just stop this," he shouted enormously.

Sumi couldn't control her laughter and she cried into lol. Deepthi laughed for a few seconds too. The operators stopped the ride. John ran to the dustbin and started vomiting.

"Dude, Are you okay? She kidded you man" Abhinav asked him.

"John, you were about to pee, I saw how nervous you were." Sumi giggled.

"Wait for a minute Sumi, I'll come and drag your curly hairs," said John.

Abhinav sensed the gaze Deepthi gave on him. It was not friendly. It was something anxious. Deepthi was always close-hearted and she was the only keeper of her heart secrets.

Every girl is not fond of assets, jewels, bank balance and royal life. They are just few. Others are the one who looks for a kind-hearted man, a cute lovely pet, a good small place to live and a romantic life to lead with their loved one.

Deepthi desired for a man like that. She knew Abhinav was a quite good one, who satisfies all good qualities of a man. He never crossed his limits and he never stopped to shoulder her in all her hard times. He made her comfortable whenever she was with him and he never took any advantage of her.

Although many girls tried to hit on him, Abhinav denied them all and waited for a true love to shower on him. *'Love is eternal· It should be felt, only from the girl you deserve·'*

Some girls are extra special. They keep all their desires, fantasies and soul stories only inside them and live a life for others especially for their families. Most of the Indian women are from the extra special category. They never cared for them, they never make food for them, they never earn for them and they never do domestic work for them.

All of them were at Chennai after a long trip to Bangalore. Most of the proposals had done, few were gone as ash, some were delighted into love and another pretty count of it were remained as silent pause buttons which continued in just friendship zone.

"C'mon just few kisses. Try this. I have seen it from Pirates of the Caribbean. I am not an Orlando Bloom, yet I have my own tactics too. Few kisses won't ruin our friendship baby," John flirted with Aparna like everytime he did with beautiful girls.

"No, I never need a guy like you," she answered.

"Not in life or for kisses," he giggled.

Sumi was watching and observing these all from a little distance. She never hated John, but his activities were the one which annoyed her the most. She was not the one to explain and lead him in a right manner, but somewhat inside her heart she had a slight affection for him.

All the time when she saw him flirting with the girls she knew it was just his time pass and he would never go deep in hurting any one's heart and soul. Although she understood it all, she didn't want to be a dumb like this. She thought she was jealous. She misjudged her own mind.

It wasn't jealousy. Being over caring or over possessive will look like being jealous. Jealousy is not that one you don't trust. Sometimes you are too much in love with that person.

Sumi knew that feelings won't die easily because we keep feeding them with memories. In fact, the feelings for John in Sumi was growing more and more since the day they met.

She liked his open talks, his straight forward mind, his take it easy policy. Behind every Casanova, there would be a Romeo or Majnu, maybe they would be dead or hurt by a severe heartbreak.

Sumi never revealed it to anyone including Deepthi. Being a rock and roll girl in college and every guy was dying for, even she had some corner in her heart. Like most of the Indian girls she came into a conclusion that 'Say it other day.'

Love is eternal

Citi Centre Mall,

Chennai

Deepthi and Abhinav were at Citi Centre Mall, Mylapore. A good program was about to be conducted. Abhinav arranged all the things for it and he personally talked with the manager in charge to conduct a program in the middle of the ground floor. "Three, Two, One …. start," Deepthi signaled him.

The speakers started to let it voices out. A guy at the corner played a mix of Indian songs and Abhinav started to dance in the center pathway of the mall. In few minutes Deepthi joined him too. And in another few minutes some joined and they all did a flash mob which gathered a pleasant number of crowd there.

After a fifteen-minute dance session, they all settled down and Abhinav took the mic and started to talk. They kept a banner of Cerebral Palsy and its effects on the body. Deepthi brought twelve people of that kind and made them to be there in the sight of the people.

"Cerebral Palsy is a disease which attacks constantly on four limbs in the body especially the legs. You are seeing the people who are affected by it and still living a life like you and me and all. It is their confidence and their handwork which endures all the happiness in their life including a normal life, their hobbies and all." He continued pointing to a girl who was in her early twenties sitting in a wheel chair.

"Meet Ms. Chandrika, a girl who is having this disease from the time of her birth and she is achieving even those which are impossible for us. She is a B.A B.L graduate who is working as a Lawyer and also writes blogs as a hobby," he pointed to another person,who wore rounded spectacles and was in his early thirties.

"He is Mr.Alfred. He was ignored by his family, when they diagnosed his inability to do his own tasks due to his illness. They left him in an orphanage and they never came to meet him. But he never lost the faith in himself. He loved himself and he tried his best to get recognized in the society. He is an MBBS graduate now and a practicing doctor in Guindy now."

Abhinav took a gap and Deepthi took the charge. "So as people you see here, they are not seeking any money, pity or sympathy from you all. They all want to live a good life like us. Being a differently abled one they suffered a lot in this society, yet they want to mingle with us and spread the love all over this world. We are keeping a sign board here with the banner. Whoever supports this program, please do a sign on that board. Thank You," as she finished, a great applause delivered by all showed a good faith in her and Abhinav's eyes.

While they are finished with it, all the volunteers of the awareness program headed homewards. Deepthi held Abhinav's hand and asked him to take her to the Starbucks. They usually go for the Phoenix MarketCity, so Deepthi opted it this time too and Abhinav said 'Yes' with a smile and no objection.

Abhinav and Deepthi were perfectly like-minded people who never made quarrel or fight. It can be understanding, respect, friendship or anything. All they knew was, they knew each other well. He cared for her a lot and she never denied it. In fact, she always desired to be with Abhinav.

Deepthi always sensed a good positive mindset whenever she was with Abhinav. Behind their arguments about the politics and the favourite player's stats in IPL the kindness and the care which resided between them ever.

"Abhinav, I want to ask you something if you don't mind. Can I?" Deepthi took a sip of her cold coffee and asked.

Usually Starbucks was too crowded, but that day it was less filled up. The reason was ADAM band performed outside the entrance of the shopping mall.

"Ya Deepthi. You never have to think whether you can ask or not. It's you not anyone."

"Sorry if I sound like an idiot. I know you for the past two years and I haven't seen you visiting a temple or church or mosque anything. Are you an atheist?"

"Of course! Deepthi. I was the double like you few years before. Never in my dreams I thought that I would hate our creator a lot." Abhinav said in a little furious tone.

Deepthi held his hand and came near to him. "So, like everyone you do have a story. Let me hear that." She insisted.

Seven years back Abhinav's family visited an orphanage. He and his parents met Sarah there. Sarah was a HIV positive kid who got the disease by her birth and diagnosed that in her age of 4. Being a single child in his family, Abhinav always wanted a sibling. As like his thought Sarah was very kind and very much attached to him and his family in a single day itself. Abhinav's parents understood the love in his eyes for the cute little child. They finished all the formalities to adopt the child and brought her home in a week. From that Abhinav was always with her and never left her. When things went good, suddenly on a day Sarah got pneumonia. Abhinav's parents took her to best medical centers and gave all the treatments they could. Due to the HIV disease in her, she had very less amount of white blood cells and it didn't able to fight well with the pneumonia. On the other hand, Abhinav went to temple daily after his school and worshiped a lot for Sarah. Finally, after 42 days of meticulous treatment Sarah was no more. She finally closed her eyes holding Abhinav's hand.

Nothing was there to match the loss of Sarah. The day he lost Sarah, was the day he lost his faith in gods and creators. It was not her fault to be born in this planet. It was not her fault to get that cruel disease by birth. It was not her fault to die in a manner like that. The agony, the pain, the tears Abhinav went through made his thoughts on God like a stone. According to him then, we should live and take care of us. Love all and care all. He was living by that in his mind.

After that he joined as a volunteer in many non-profit organizations to help the people and the orphanages as much he could.

A single stream of tear rolled from his eye. Deepthi took a tissue and rubbed her tears in that and passed another one to Abhinav. She was speechless, yet she rubbed his palm over his hand and consoled him.

"We never knew the birth date of Sarah. But she always wanted to celebrate it on Feb 29. She proudly said that she was special so that her birthday will come once in four years rather than on every year like others. But in 2010 she stopped her heartbeats," Abhinav added and looked into Deepthi's eyes.

Deepthi opened her arms and hugged him. He cried a lot on her shoulder. She tried to console him a lot. Amidst of agony one should never see the place or people whom they are with, they will simply let their feelings out.

Men are always Men

George University,

Chennai

"Deepthi, can you listen to me and give me a suggestion for my problem?" Sumi asked Deepthi.

Deepthi looked puzzled. "Am not the girl to deal with relationship issues as you know. Girls call me nerd and guys call me useless beauty. So, do you really think that I can help you?"

"Geek, how do you know it's kind of relationship issues? Did I blurt anytime in sleep?" Sumi asked with a shock.

"Ha ha. No no. Every time I am the one who ask you about before some decisions I take. You are the expert in the ideas. But now you are looking confused and asking all that to me, right? That's why I guessed it so. Wait a sec.... Are you in love?"

Sumi blushed a lot. Sumi was too modern and beyond the cultural limits. She always loved to keep her beautiful and sexy as she liked. Being a 5'4 foot, she had a perfect shape and lovely looks which every men longed. She never noticed the guys who let their jaw down and flow their saliva to the ground. Despite all her strong and hard walled heart, there existed a soft corner.

"Am I seeing it real. Let me pinch you darling." Deepthi pinched her cheek with an utter wonder.

"Ya Deepthi. But kindly don't ask whom the guy he is. I melt for him and I indicate my love for him every time I can. But that dumb head is always playful and crazy. Friendship was my choice. But falling in love was the way destiny played with my feelings."

Deepthi couldn't believe her own ears. She never saw Sumi talking so patiently and firmly about all these romantic things before. She could openly talk about the body of Sharukh Khan and how she longed for a man to show a six pack body like that. But never in her dreams Deepthi thought that Sumi would be dragged in a love like this.

And she sensed the love which was flowing in her veins drastically. On the other hand, she didn't know that John was that guy who took the lover girl of Sumi out.

Things always happen with a reason. Sometimes fate fuck us. Sometimes our own ego fuck us. But these two must never happen in love. Love is from hearts, not from the brains. Care is the only catalyst to make the love reaction happens.

John and Akash entered the 'Thalapakatti Biryani Restaurant' for dinner. Seated on their respective chairs, they ordered two mutton biryani with a half pepper barbeque chicken.

"Did you taste the onion raita here dude. It's awesome. I usually come here to have a good biriyani with lot of onion raita," Akash seems to be desperate for onion raita.

"I haven't called you here for that Akash. I want to talk about Sumi. However, Abhinav is my best friend, I feel shy to talk to him about our close friend. I think I am in love with her." Akash never expected this. Sumi, Deepthi, Abhinav, John was a gang of four who always felt like a four horsemen gang. They cared for each other. They were there every time when anyone get hurt. Apart from that, a new love seed sprouted into a small herb now inside John's chest and John continued.

"I have sensed the love in her eyes. But still she hadn't expressed it to me in words. Before all these, I had no problem to talk with her looking into her eyes. But now it's hard for me to face her gaze.

The mascara over her cute lovely eyes is killing me. Every time when I start talking with her I feel some shivering in my words. I have flirted with many girls but all the sudden I have stopped it all before eight months. It is all because of her. She came into me and she completely turned me around."

"So, are you about to propose her?" Akash asked.

"I am having a fear inside me Akash. I did many things in front of her which a man could never do in his life time. I flirted a lot with Aparna and Madhumitha. Even I asked kisses from Aparna. I talked about the transparent strap of Madhumitha's inner garment. Everything I did was infront of her. Will she accept me even after that? Will she feel the same what am currently up to? I can never guess the answers. By the way it should be our conversation. Don't let it out." Akash added.

In the meantime, the food was prepared and served to them. They had a good dinner, with a heavy load inside the stomach. But John was in the thoughts of Sumi, who was completely filled inside his heart.

People usually say that emotions are only for girls and men are always strong and more than strong enough. It is just a saying to show that men are superior. But deep inside every man's heart, there should be several untold stories. Men are good at hiding things and especially at feelings.

Also, men are proud to be like this. Actually, they never let their thoughts out when the time is in their side. After every time they are hurt by emotions, they will howl like a night owl in their sleep.

When a man has a heartbreak, his night will tell how much tales he says about his relationship. When a man has a heartbreak, his pillow will say how it rained last night. When a man has a heartbreak, his eyes will say how he control his tears and let his smile out. True or not, men are always men.

An Unusual Proposal

George University,

Chennai

Final semester of their engineering came. As a final year student John and Abhinav wanted to celebrate this time symposium like a grand one. The college supported them with a good budget. John and his fellow guys talked with few sponsors for the symposium. For up to 180 colleges, the symposium poster was sent.

Students were united to do this huge. They looked for the celebrities' names to invite them. Abhinav was the coordinator of that symposium and Akash assisted him. Deepthi was declared as the event coordinator for 'Paper Presentation', Sumi for 'Gaming', John for 'Treasure Hunt' and Abhinav for 'Best Manager.'

The feelings for John inside her heart killed Sumi a lot. Sumi wanted to hug him, kiss him and tell him how she felt and fell for him.

"Is that a desire? Is that an urge? No, it's not. It is a form of love. The love every living being in this planet die for. The love where nightingale sings for its pair at lone nights."

"So, when you are going to tell him everything? Time is not always by our side dear," Deepthi said Sumi touching her head with her fingers.

Friends are never like relatives. They won't mourn for your loss like relatives, instead they will do everything they can do to keep you good. They won't just shed their sympathy on you like your relatives, friends are those who would take all their share even in your hardness as the thorn.

Friends are the ones who look a job for you after your graduation, despite of just telling about to get a job.

Deepthi studied Sumi well. She knew it was her periods when she shouts at her like a hell. And she knew how could she shower the friendship love on her. Inspite of being friends, they were sisters. John was looking for the perfect time to express his love for Sumi. The fear about getting rejected grew bigger and bigger in heart.

But letting everything happens as it in its way is not the human way. One should face it, rule it and make it to themselves and write the history of it

The Symposium organizers named it as 'AMOANZ 2K13'. A grand stage was built in the auditorium to seat the dignitaries on the floor and the performance to be done during the symposium.

Deepthi worked on the small water tank to look it like an android. The holes were put in the sides and two small pipes were pasted there. Green color was painted and it looked exactly like an android on its finish.

Sumi gathered juniors to make the publicity via social networks. They posted the official posters of AMOANZ 2K13 in the college groups and technical pages on Facebook and Instagram.

John looked Sumi from a distance. She was busy with a pen on head her with a rectangular specs on her ears. The rose-colored frame bent sharply over her ears and seated very well. Though she was very much concentrated in the computer, her forehead wrinkles and the curvy eyebrows of her eyes added her beauty too. She bit the bottom tip of the pen in her hand often.

John looked her without a blink. He slowly started moving near her. He stood exactly few inches at the back of her. He admired how beautiful she was. Her hair was neatly spread over her shoulders. The petals designed purple tops she wore gave a nice match for the bracelet she put on her right hand. Her shoulders to hand he saw the flawless skin of her and admired her beauty a lot.

Without saying anything he left the place. Abhinav saw this and went back to his task with a smile over his lips.

"Who are the sponsors you got Abhinav?" his college Principal asked.

"Sir, we have talked with almost 24 companies. In that we got 7 sponsors. Tiago Motors is the big company who sponsored about 80,000 rupees. And they want to keep their newly arrived bike models in our symposium events."

"Good one Abhinav. Make this event adorable. All the Best."

"We'll do our best,sir" Abhinav replied.

On the last week, Saturday morning at 9 Am, the symposium was inaugurated. Followed by the National Anthem and welcome speech other events were conducted.

"Everything is going good. Let it make a great success for our batch." Sumi whispered in Abhinav's ears who stood near to her.

"Love takes a moment to fall into, and it takes a life to get out from Sumi. Think about it." Abhinav whispered back. Goosebumps hit her body as she heard that from Abhinav. Not showing that all she turned to him.

"I think John is in love with some girl." Abhinav told. As these words went into her ears, she stood still unknowing what to do next. Even though she was curious and eager enough to know whom the girl was, she was broken at heart. For the first time, it pained her when she longed for John in her heart.

She took a gulp of water from the Bisleri bottle she had and she blinked her eyes and started breathing faster. The next event to be conducted was "The Best Manager."

John was one of the contestants with the four others. In Best Manager event, one should act like what the task given to them and act naturally to the situation mentioned with it. For the first contestant, a girl from Mepco Schlenk Engineering College, the task was 'To act like a Soap Sales Manager to the dealers'.

The girl was slightly shocked to get a task like this, but gaining courage she did a good act like 'It was a Hanshika's favorite soap and she is using it for a long.' She got a good applause.

Abhinav indicated John as the next contestant. The whole auditorium heard the name of John when he walked towards the stage. After all he was the Cassanova of the college. Happiness filled in the air. AMAONZ 13 was the most expected celebration of that whole year after their industrial visit.

Sumi stood near the Air cooler kept beside the Big speaker on the left of the stage in 30 feet distance from it. She wore a green long gown with a satin silk pink belt on her waist. She had a Marigold flower on her head just above her left ear. Sumi looked gorgeous in that gown.

John never stopped looking her directly. He admired her beauty inch by inch. Most of the times he skipped his beats in her veins of the love he had in his eyes.

Love is like 'Mutual Fund Investments are subject to the Market Risk· Please Read offered document carefully'· Before you could welcome it in your heart, it will get rid of your brain and talk from your heart, intentionally putting you upside down and will melt you as much it can·

As like that, John was changed utterly. He had to prove that he was once a Casanova and he was not the same then. He felt the love flowing from his love glands and desperately wanted to be with Sumi every second of his life.

Even Sumi was same though, but still she hesitated and stopped herself to let John vomit all his feelings on her. And she thought almost that she was one who died for his feelings and she never knew how John felt too.

A tricky task came to John. He had to act by the scene they gave. He looked confused whether he could do it or not. The task was, 'Your friend is loving a girl for so long and she never knew it before. So, you take your friend to her and tell his feelings to her. All of a sudden, she likes you and proposes you in instant. What would you do? Act like that.'

John was thinking for some time, how he could do it and what mannerism he should perform. He was ready and about to start. He made a quick look of the auditorium and the people who were present there to see his performance.

Amidst of all he got Sumi by her looks. She stood there pleasantly, her hands were cross and standing like a princess in her castle's balcony. John made up his mind to do something different.

He realized chances won't knock our heart always, we should grab it once it comes for us.

The whole auditorium was silent and he started to speak. Sumi was smiling towards him and it killed him a lot. He held the microphone and constantly gazed at Sumi. Whenever he looked into her eyes, he lost himself in her. The only thing he believed ever is, 'Anyone can be with him, but she must be the girl who will complete him'.

"My love, we have our own scribbled writings in our heart for each other so long. But I don't want to make that like as it as in the upcoming days. Whenever I am with you, whenever you look at me, whenever you constantly look into my eyes, whenever you give a funny expression with your tongue on your nose, whenever you mischievously mocking me, a strange feeling has grown into me. Initially I took it as common, as a male urge over a woman. Day by day your thoughts started killing me.

I was a good friend to you and am still. Never in my dreams I thought that I will be in love with my bestie - you. It happened. I said it again honey, it happened. You are in my senses. *I can have a girl in future, but I won't be complete when it is not you.*

I had an idea to jump off this stage and come straightly to you for proposing my feelings in the crowd. But I resisted myself a lot. Because, I have a slight disturbance in my mind whether you feel the same like me or not. Due to that, I haven't told all this before.

I know I was not a one girl guy before, I swear I won't be like that ever in my life if I am with you. You are the show light of my life, you are the dignity of my life. *I want to kiss your feet and comb your hair daily up to the day I die in your lap.*

I want to hold your hands in public proudly when I take you for shopping, for dinner, for having vodka silently at woods secretly at nights as my soul mate. I might be an option for you. But you are the girl I deserve.

I don't want to bore you more as you know am not too emotional like this before. I love you honey. I love you the most in this planet. Come and combine with me, my soul and my life."

The people gathered in that auditorium was amused. It was not by his performance, by his proposal to Sumi. She stood shocked and confused. She never thought John had so much feelings inside him. As of then, all the people of their college knew John as a playful guy who was a take it easy guy ever. But she saw with her own eyes.

It was not the cheater's voice. It was not the voice of a lusty guy. It was the desperate voice of a guy who proposed to his girl in a big stage. And she was confused about his feelings. John wasn't mentioned her name while he talked.

Sumi was really upset. She didn't know it was her that John poured out his words out for. Sumi ran to her class and sat in the last bench and dug her face in her hands. In stage, John was eliminated to the wrong performance he did other than the given one. He might be eliminated, but he won many hearts there. He saw Sumi running towards their classroom. He stepped down from the stage and informed Abhinav that he need some time alone. Abhinav patted his shoulders and sent him. John started walking towards the class, where the whole college was empty and all were inside the auditorium.

John opened the door and walked in silently. Sumi was there resting her head on the bag kept over the desk. John went near her and sat only inches away from her. She didn't respond as she didn't know that he was there. Even the classroom can be a castle, if the king and queen are in love.

He touched her hair fondly. Sumi got up and saw him. She rubbed the tears over her eyes with the napkin.

"Hey, I.... I just saw your proposal. I am happy for you and the girl you proposed. By the way you hided it from me so long." She told in a mild tone.

John went too close to her. He could sense her hot breath and the smell of her perfume. There was no one around them. The two swans were alone with their feelings on each other. He touched her cheeks slowly and felt the softness of it. Her skin was so soft, as he saw her skin turned red when he rubbed it slowly with his thumb.

Sumi realized everything. She came to know for whom John let all the feelings out. She was waiting gladly with her eyes on his eating him fully for his move.

"Meeting you was fate, becoming your friend was a choice, but falling in love with you was beyond my control. You are my everything, Sumi."

She held her right arm firmly. "I never knew before that I am the girl for you. But I know I am the girl you deserve, to spend the days and nights with me and am in your love every minute of my life. There are only two times that I want to be with you.... Now and Forever." she whispered.

John was really happy for her words. He felt the complete love in a girl's eyes and it was from Sumi. She rested her hands on his shoulder and hugged him. John looked at her lips desperately. She had a mild coat of pale shiny pink lipstick which gave a perfect finish on her lips. It looked juicy and it invited him a lot. They were feeling that for the first time.

He tilted his head slightly and perceived the aroma of her lips with his nose. Sumi was eagerly expecting that. She made him comfortable by sitting cross legged and very near to him with her arms on his shoulders.

John planted his lips on her deliberately. He tried the flavor of his lips and started licking it. Sumi opened her lips and provoked him to taste her mouth. She wanted this badly from the day she had feelings on him. John evoked his tongue touched hers. He nibbled her tongue and took a savor of her saliva. She shut her eyes and enjoyed the smooch. They were tightly coupled with the embrace.

John got going to every nook and corner of it. He had the thought that she was his girl and she was his only girl. He bit her lower lip and pulled it. Sumi moaned in a low tone as John kissed it badly.

He stopped biting and he said "If I could be anything I would be your tear, so I could be born in your eyes, live down your cheek and die on your lips."

My Drug??? Her Smile!

Kulfi House,

Chennai

It had been a week since they both were in a relationship. John and Sumi invited Deepthi, Abhinav and Akash over for an evening snacks. It was the Saturday evening, so everybody was available.

Deepthi came in a black border zebra patterned poonam saree with an excellent dark red color blouse matching her bindi. As usual she had a very less makeup. She had her hair combed in the traditional way which fall neatly to her waist. Abhinav was wearing a black cotton kurta with ivory color pyjamas.

Kulfis for all arrived. "To the new love couple." Akash threw his hand in the air. "Happy for you my darling." Deepthi expressed happily.

John put an arm over her shoulder and Sumi gave a peck on his cheeks. That was lovely. Abhinav was very happy to see John like this. From being like a pervert, he was a responsible man of a girl's love then. A 180-degree turn happened in his life. Sumi was the perfect girl to take care of his all naughtiness only for her and make him sleep in her arms with lots and lots of love.

Deepthi went to some distance as she got a call from her dad.

"Haan... Appa, how are you? How is mom and all?"

"Everyone is fine dear. We are going to attend our caste society meeting. Our caste leader wants everyone to come with their whole family. It's on coming Thursday."

"But Appa. It's up to your generation. Am not interested in these kinds of things and you know that."

"As you are educated, you can throw this tradition and culture ma. But you have to never demolish the culture you came from. You have to keep that in mind."

"Education gives equality. And am tired of explaining it to know. Anyway, you people go, I have some work here in college."

"Mmm. You have to change. It's must for your future."

"Appa, leave it. I know what to do. Am not a kid." She cut the call. Her family was based from a South Tamil Nadu village. Her family was very honored by their caste. But apart from that Deepthi was different. She believed always that love, kindness and care are the ones which leads to humanity.

She returned back with a smile. Abhinav felt something strange inside. He never saw Deepthi so beautiful before. He knew that she was beautiful, but the new look of her in saree destroyed his innocence. He gazed at her with the side corner of his eyes. He admired how she smile and raise her eyebrow while talking. Intentionally he was getting addicted to her presence with him.

According to Abhinav ' Some people say Love is cute when it's new. But I believe love is most beautiful when it's last.' Abhinav can see something more beautiful in her eyes and smile than the stars.

They all had two more kulfis for each and another which the love couple had.

"What are your plans for today guys? It's Saturday night. Can we go for the Continental Cuisine for dinner?"

"Ufff... No John. I am going to visit the Hanuman Temple tomorrow," Deepthi said with a delight.

"Ok Deepthi. So, what about you, Akash?"

"No yaar. You two have a nice romantic night. I don't want to be an elephant between you. And the main reason is I will get jealous when looking you both." He winked at John. Everyone laughed and they left for the day.

Deepthi asked Abhinav to drop her in her hostel as Sumi was not her company right then. Abhinav drove her and let her reach the hostel. She got down and started walking towards her hostel. Her foot petals touched the ground and her anklet beads gave a good tone for his ears. He was there observing that all. She stopped in few steps and turned towards him.

"You look pretty handsome in Kurta, Abhinav. It suits you well."

"Thanks, Deepthi. By the way yours is a nice combination and drew many eyes on you in the last one hour."

"Don't make me blush." She smiled.

"I will be alone tomorrow for temple. Can you accompany me if you are free?"

"Always there for you Deepthi." He said and gave a little smile.

"Sari. Come in Shirt and Dhoti then." She winked. And Abhinav loved it.

They were at the Hanuman Temple at Nanganallur, Chennai. It is a famous one in the Chennai city. You can see thousands and thousands of people worshipping in front of the big and finely carved figure of Hanuman.

Deepthi wore a yellow-gold silk saree. It had the silver-plated beads on the border of it. She had a bunch of jasmine buds tied in a thin wool thread. She had a saffron bindi on her forehead and she looked awesome. She was too traditional. It was her. It was Deepthi. She never tried to gain attention of Abhinav. But it was never missed.

She was drastically killing Abhinav with her beauty. She never exposed it, but she always gained his attention towards it. Abhinav was in a pink silk shirt with a silk dhoti as Deepthi opted. He was merely handsome, as Deepthi never missed to notice.

"It had been years since I visited a temple after the death of Sarah," Abhinav said.

"So, you are finally back because of me. Thanks, Abhinav."

"You don't need to mention it Deepthi. As I said, I'll be always there for you." He smiled and she did too.

As she planned to worship every corner and worship places, Abhinav stood near pillar leaning on it. With his hands crossed he looked down, where he was the only man there among all the women crowd. He was never shy with Deepthi, but Deepthi saw him so shy to others then.

Boys who lower their eyes while passing by a girl are really so cute and adorable. He remained there patiently when Deepthi took minutes to perform pooja. She liked all the characteristics of Abhinav. Plenty of guys could come and go, but Abhinav was different.

Deepthi was much friendlier to him than others. And Abhinav was very much attached to Deepthi as all the folks in the college knew. Deepthi tried to introduce him to her family. But she didn't know how they take it. They never considered a boy and girl as friends.

Among these all Deepthi was too casual with him. After the temple, Abhinav took her to Sangeetha Restaurant for the meals. She observed how manly he was. Being six feet tall, and in good figure, he might have had many girls as much as possible. But he never thought in his dreams about that.

He was a one-girl man, who believed deeply in love. They left from the hotel to her hostel. Back in the room, Deepthi was changed into pink sleeveless and white shorts. She opened her secret mail and started typing.

To the man of my smile and blush,

I know you always take care of me, doing things for me, making me smile everyday as a friend. Even I felt the same before, but I am not that one now. I don't know whether it is just a friendship or more than that. I don't know still whether the same feelings comes into your mind as well as mine. As, I sit here and think about you and what you and I have been through, I see that I can only love you more and more with each passing day. You're my inspiration each and every day. You are what keeps me going when I just want to give up. You are the one who hold my hands and instruct me in most of the things in my life. I smell in near future, you are gonna be my reason of living.

I love the way you care about me. I love the way you look gently into my eyes. I love the way you come closer and kiss me in my dreams. I wouldn't know where to turn if I didn't have you. You are this girl's dream, which she desires to be true.

I wish you could feel all the passion and all the love I carry around for you. You have won my heart and soul. You have won it all already. You make me feel like I am in heaven, in the arms of an angel whenever am with you. You and I must have a fulfilling relationship and I swear I must be the one you deserve. As it goes on, I wonder which is it?? friends or lovers? That is not specific yet. We've been friends for four long years now, but this friendship isn't just that anymore, at least for me. I have fallen in love with you, and I need to tell you that I am your soul mate masquerading as a good friend.

I noticed today when we were at the temple, how you were there. Leaning on the pillars and stood like an innocent one with the trimmed beard and the fascinating eyes looking down on the floor. You stood still like a kid kept between all the elders of this world unknowing what to do. I really loved the way you stood there. You were damn adorable. In fact, my hands were up to give a small pinch on your cheeks, but the woman inside me stopped doing that. I dream daily about you. You and me in a beach, looking towards the full moon, holding your hands, hearing the voices of the tides, with the breeze on our lips, with no one around us. Will it happen in real?

Will I get the same from you? Or will I lose you from my life forever? I think I can keep masquerading as a good friend till our last breath. I can lose my love, but any cost I won't lose you from my life. I want you to be my side always. Forever in my life, I need to be in your arms. My heart wants us to be soul mates but my brain says 'Let's stay as friends'. What should I do?

Am I going to click pictures on your wedding, with the other girl whom you don't deserve more than me. Will I be alive at the exact moment that happens? May be only physically I guess.

I can erase all the feelings I have for you, but Memories... they won't die.

your Ravishing Bae.

Saved this in draft, she closed the mail as she closed her heart from pouring out all the voices of it to Abhinav.

The next day Abhinav was in class, where he couldn't find John and Sumi. He looked out for them and they weren't there. Akash told that they left for the 'Chennai Express' movie in Luxe Cinemas, Phoenix Marketcity. As he searched for Deepthi, she was also absent for the day. During break, he called Deepthi's phone number and she took the call.

"Deepthi, where are you yaar? Are you coming for classes today?"

"No Abhinav. Am sick totally. I can't come and I have my assignments pending. Inform Lecturer Mathangi that I'll submit it tomorrow."

"Ok no problem, I'll let her know that. But you are alone there. Sumi left with John for the film. Do you need any help? Can I take you to the hospital?"

"It's not that big Abhinav. I just have some stomach ache and am out of meds. I tried to call Sumi but as you said she is in theater she couldn't have heard her phone ringing."

"Ok. Stay there. I'll be there in ten minutes."

"But Abhinav..." as she continued, she came to know that the call was no more. Abhinav departed from the college and took his bike to the hostel.

He reached her hostel as soon as possible and he signed the visitor's attendance. Abhinav walked to Deepthi's room. Deepthi was resting in the bed with one hand pressing lightly on her stomach. He could feel the pain she went through.

Deepthi welcomed Abhinav and tried to get up, but due to the over pain in her stomach she wasn't able to make it properly. Abhinav made her comfortable on the bed and rubbed her fore head lightly.

"Are you having fever with pain in the stomach?"

"No Abhinav, I am in my periods and as I said I forgot the date. I am out of my meds. That's the problem."

"Mmm. Why did you keep silent and haven't made a call to me?"

"But Abhinav it's a girl thing. I thought you weren't quite knowing about it."

"See Deepthi, it is the thing what all the girls have in their life for years. And still people are thinking bad to talk this in public. Society is for us, we are not for society." He continued.

"Give me twenty minutes. I will be back with the medicines and some food for you." and he left. Deepthi gave a smile as she knew he was the perfect man for a girl.

Abhinav was back with Aspirin tablets, a half litres ofBovonto, two stay-free secure napkins pack and a box of breakfast with gulab jamuns.

She loved the way he took care of her. He was there with her throughout the day, helping her and doing things for her.

Most of the time he was at the veranda, plugged in with music in is smartphone and surfing through the internet. Often, he came into her room to check whether she was alright. And it was 8 pm, he started to his place, as he bid a bye to Deepthi.

Deepthi took her laptop and started composing her secret mail.

To the man of my smile and blush,

When last and first time I saw you cried in my shoulders for Sarah was the time I came to know how pretty you are with emotions. I consoled you on the other day, but you came in my world with no excuses. You are a perfect man whom a girl should marry and desire of. I came through many men in this world. Among them, some were ugly at their heart. And some of them had no respect for woman. But I felt the freedom, love, care, happiness everything overloaded when am with you.

Today when you are with me, looking for my health and taking care of me you marked whom you are with. I felt very special in your hands when I was with you in a whole single day as your bestie. I never know, if the feelings for me will lures inside you. But I hope I will get all the ones I deserve from you. You came in my life like a King and you are ruling inside me. Let this princess be your queen at your lap always. Will you say once you feel it? Or will you wait until I express it to you? Time is a master and it plays well in people lives. A great congo for it.

your Ravishing Bae.

Collision of Supremacy

George University Auditorium,

Chennai.

The college day celebration was yet to start. Everyone was gathered inside the auditorium and the people were in joy. Sumi and John were in the backstage. The performance by Sumi was about to happen.

Sumi was a classical dancer and an expert in Bharathanatyam. She was in a white classical costume for dance. She had worn the ornaments on her forehead, nose, ears and arms. A pair of golden anklets was in her legs.

John hugged and wished her. He told her how much he was expecting to see her performance on stage. Deepthi was with Abhinav in the front row to see the dance.

Sumi kissed John in lips and walked to the stage. John went to sit with Deepthi and Abhinav. Sumi started dancing for 'Jiya Jale – Dil Se'. John loved the swings she danced. She was dancing in the part of a desperate solo girl who dances in the thoughts of her dream lover.

Within no time a chair flew from the air and fell down in the foot of Abhinav. Everyone was shocked and Sumi stopped her dance. A fight broke out between Mechanical and ECE department students. In the middle of the arena there was only four ECE students and they were surrounded by the mass crowd of Mechanical department people.

Deepthi ran to the stage and took Sumi down from the stage. John hurried them to leave the place and Abhinav started sending all the faculties and women from the arena. A serious fight came up in no second.

The mech boys started throwing chairs on the ECE guys. They protected themselves shielding the chair by having it in their hand. Chairs were in the air like the arrows shot from the bow during the war.

Sumi and Deepthi reached their classroom safely. Sumi started crying and Deepthi consoled her. Abhinav and John tried to cool down the situation, but they weren't successful in that. The mech students have thrown all other people out and started beating the four ECE students. Prathesh, from final year ECE took a chair in his hand and started swinging it in air. Suddenly a head caught in between of the chair and he dragged it to the ground. Amidst of all the beatings on him, he stomped him hard in his head. In the meantime, police arrived and everything came into control.

John made a phone call with Sumi and Deepthi near the Computer Lab which was at the second floor of the Main Block. They opened the door and came out.

Abhinav came when others were coming out and put his palm on Deepthi's shoulder. Her eyes were blurred as soon she felt a palm over her shoulder. She started fainting and went weak. Deepthi went unconscious.

Sumi, John and Abhinav were at the Fortis Hospital, Adyar. Doctors informed them that she fainted of sudden fear she felt. Sumi and John left Deepthi with Abhinav and went to collect the medicines at the pharmacy and to settle the bill.

Abhinav went inside the ward. Deepthi was weak and sat with a little struggle. They were silent for some time, until Abhinav started first.

"Did you felt that again?" Abhinav asked.

Tears evoked from Deepthi's eyes as she remembered everything happened that night.

It all happened that night. . .

Three years before. A night with a light breeze and she was walking just by admiring the beauty of the creamy full moon in the sky. On the day, before one hour she went to her schoolmate Nisha's residence and appealed a divorce for her friend who wanted to get rid of her drunkard husband. Nisha's mother was always fond of Deepthi and she never stopped the care Deepthi showed on Nisha even in her personal life issues. Trust is like gold, it is noble always.

Deepthi informed Abhinav about her visit to Nisha's home and she could return on her own. So, Abhinav remained with his friends. Nisha was married in her early seventeen where she was from a poor family. Her husband was an impotent and he never touched his blossom wife. To remain good in society, he married her and his family supported him everytime.

Despite being in fear, Nisha overcame many difficulties in her life. From her father's death atthe age of five to getting married at seventeen. Although, Nisha's mom had no interest in that, she had no choice too. On her first night, Nisha visited her decorated room and what she had seen was her man having spirit and pickles. She lost the interest in marriage and lived like a living corpse.

She did domestic works and as usual like every housewife, her husband made her work like a servant day by day and he went cheap. One of his fine day, he made an oral agreement with the landlord of his place. He finalized the deal of 2 lakh Indian rupees for Nisha's Virginity. He came home and he chanted it loudly in front of her. "Money... Nisha.... Money...". Nisha was scattered and helpless. Being a poor girl in her teens, she worried why God created all the problems in her life. In fact, she was a gem, who should be in a guy's arms as petals. But she was there like utensils which was used only when it was needed.

He brought him home and the landlord tipped him with a generous smile over his face. Her husband grinned and made a way to let them alone inside the walls surrounded. That guy came near to her and touched her belly. She looked him with a shock and tears flooded from her eyes. Despite of considering it, he started tasting her shoulder and tore the back of her blouse like a hungry wolf preying on a fresh meat. Nisha was poor in life too, she begged to leave her.

But the animal's ears didn't hear it and almost went down to grab her legs. She couldn't withstand up that. She found the pile of bottles over the corner of the living room. Pushed him to the door, she hit him hard with the glass bottle on his head and in his balls. He howled in pain and he fell down with a stream of blood from his head.

Nisha sat there motionless. After three hours, her mom came and saw this devastation and took her to hospital. She filed a rape case on the landlord and called Deepthi by phone. Deepthi arrived shortly and consoled her. She also told her mom that she would be alright.

When they both heard the things happened, they initially went to the women's' welfare lawyer, who was damn good in these types of social cases. Ms. Usha Jaganath was a gold medalist from Rajiv Gandhi Law University, Chennai and practicing as a Legal advisor for women's problems in society. She filed the complaint and they were waiting for the divorce.

Nisha's mom brought dosas and mutton curry to Deepthi and Nisha. Deepthi missed her family a lot. She was very much attached to Nisha and her mom. After some minutes of talk, she left to her hostel. Nisha's mom came to accompany her up to bus stand, but she denied it with a smile.

"With a smartphone, you can come around the world aunty. Let me go and take care of my dear a lot. Love you both. See you."

She started walking to the bus stand. Due to some works on the road, the path was diverted. The GPS, which she trusted a lot, screwed her. Turning right to the street she saw a parallel road and she went by that. Finally, she stuck in the middle of a light dark area and tried to call Abhinav. Her mobile had no network coverage and everything was pissed off completely.

Deepthi was brave and she started walking towards the path she came from. Within some seconds of time, she heard a sound, which was from a bike coming near to her. She had a hope and expected it to stop near her. A man in his early 40's got down from the bike and stood in front of her. Before she could open her mouth, he did and left her stood shocked and stunned.

"Seven thousand rupees, final rate for the night. I have a safe place and I have rubbers for our protection." He said with a sly smile.

No reply came from her. She was in an absolute state where her heart stopped beating and brain stopped working. She started sweating badly and the drops fell rapidly to the ground.

' People do talk about women empowerment, welfare and rights. But this whole society is a shit, which have all the shit eaters in this planet. ' She thought in her mind. She tried to explain him a lot. He didn't make any effort to hear that. All he wanted was to enter her.

Like most of the abusive men in this world, he was starving like a bitchy dog searching for a decayed bone from dustbin for sex.

"Hello, don't worry. I won't be so rude. Just for a night and the pleasure is mutual. Pretend like a whore not a kid. Looks like a fresher but whores remain whores not goddess." He spitted his harsh words with the lusty eyes.

She knew that won't get over until she cleared him out. "I came here by wrong direction mistakenly shown by my GPS. Trust me am not a whore and am a student."

He never minded it all. Her beauty and her situation of being alone gave some more confidence to him.

"C'mon. Don't act like a virgin. I know you bitches are clever foods for your Professor's lust. Why don't I taste you in such terms? Add me in that list too." He said in a strong tone.

Pain is not the one which tears your physical strength, it is the knife to put a nice deep cut over your heart and makes you to lose all your mental strength and fucks your brains out.

It was the state which every female in the society faces, where no girl baby, girl child, girl, woman, mom and even a granny can't walk in the road alone. They will get raped, abused. Or they will be grabbed and taken to some dark areas to satisfy the lusty male meat of some human animal's sex thirst.

She turned south and started walking. He followed her. Tears broke out from her eyes and it started shedding from its corner. She couldn't turn back and she was helpless. Within a fraction of second, she felt a palm on her shoulder.

He rubbed her shoulders and touched her arms. As a pervert, he wanted to enter her immediately and he grabbed her left hand and tried to bury his face in her neck. She pushed him and tried to run away from her.

He caught her shawl, surrounded over her neck and pulled her. Grabbing her hair, he slapped her once on her right cheek. Her lip got a wound and blood came out. She fainted and went unconscious.

He looked her like a pleasure toy made of flesh and went near to her. He was at right top of her. Looking towards her neck he wanted to get satisfied from his urge. He went closer to lick her neck. He was inches apart.

A punch came from right to his jaw which tore his bottom lip, when he felt it. He fell on the ground and looked for where it came from. Abhinav stood there with a furious look in her eyes.

Before he could react, Abhinav slapped furiously on his cheek and wherever he could. He tried to defense it and wasn't able to block it of being in the ground. Abhinav took a wooden branch and beat him like hell. He had strips on his back, while Abhinav whipped his beats on him badly. He screamed in pain and he stood back.

Abhinav was in no mood to leave him. He wanted to kill him and make him rot in hell. With a huge strength, he punched him right down of his abdomen, as he felt his hand gripped punch felt like a leather ball hitting through the abdomen. He was almost torn and went bad. After some minutes of all the mess, Abhinav took her to the hospital in his bike and admitted her.

"How did you come there? No one knew I was there."

"I was searching for you for some minutes, Deepthi. Roamed through all the streets. But couldn't find you. Atlast, I found you in the bastard's thirst."

She slightly got up and leaned on the wall. He couldn't see her like that. He offered her a wheat sandwich and she denied it.

"Thanks. I mustn't live if something happened there." She said with drops of tears. He rubbed it with a napkin.

"Virginity is not in body Deepthi. It should be in souls. It should always shower all the love you have only to the soul mate you deserve." He said and left the room.

After three years, she had that faint again by the feeling of palm over her shoulders suddenly. Abhinav consoled her and she relaxed. Sumi and John returned back as Abhinav went to get lunch for them all.

The Rooftop Dinner

"Can you handle the pressure good? Because it's an IT job. You may get constant stress mostly in this most growing industry. Take your time and let us know." Mr. Ramnath, HR of Joltron Tech Limited asked Abhinav.

"Sir, I have no doubt in that. For your kind information, I completed Engineering." He replied with a smile on his face.

Mr. Ramnath announced the people list he selected for his company. With three more members Abhinav got the offer letter for him too. And Deepthi was not in the plan to enter in the IT firm as she always said "I never want to lose my hair and my hobbies."

She planned to join one of the finest bank exams coaching center in Chennai. Even his father didn't love his daughter working and wanted her to get married soon. So, he can be relieved from one of his duties.

"So, what's John going to do next?" asked Deepthi.

"Sounds like taking care of his Father's Hotel business. He wanted to make his son as M.D of his concerns." Sumi replied with proud in her eyes.

"Mmm... Sounds interesting too. Going to grab beers or going to Punjabi Nation?"

"Hey... Don't remind about alcohol just now in the morning itself. It's for nights."

"Aahaan..." Deepthi giggled.

Sumi applied a little makeup and an emerald necklace which John gifted for her birthday a month before. She wore a black single piece dress which fitted good on her up to her neck to her knees with a full sleeve. It was glittery and she had a dark red lip stick on her lips looked so cute for her dress.

She wore black stockings with the red shiny high heel shoes. She ordered a cab and it was arrived.

"To the Azzuri Bay Restaurant, Adyar." She guided the taxi driver.

John always wanted to pick her up with his 320d M Sport variant BMW. But she always preferred to be in her own hands. She was arrived and opened the door of the restaurant.

"Sumi... Am here." John waved his hand in the air. They exchanged smiles and she sat opposite to him.

He was in blue and yellow checked shirt with black jeans and casual sneakers for the meet. He trimmed his beard so nicely and it showed the perfect lining connecting the French beard to his moustache.

John noticed Sumi a lot. He started her eyes looking to the menu card as her hand neatly brushing her hairs and the way she looked that card, biting her lips as she got all the focus of him towards her.

She ordered Roasted Chicken Soup and Lemon Fish as starters followed by Spicy Chicken Mozzarella Italian thin crust pizza for the main course.

The waiter served their order and left the table. John held her right hand in his hands.

"So, this guy here pretends to be romantic. You people know he was a Cassanova," She told it aloud.

John looked her firmly with a small fake anger in his eyes. Everyone in the restaurant giggled as she said that.

"Why Sumi? I was not like that before, you know that darling."

"Oh! my sweet honey.... I said you were not you are," She winked.

And they chatted about their upcoming first anniversary and how they can celebrate.

"Shall we go for Ooty? It must be lovable," John suggested.

"Acchaa…you are planning to wear me for the chill climate there." She laughed.

"No, No... May be we can enjoy our days with some spice." He added and gave a naughty smile.

Life gives multiple options in many things, except love. Love is not just a word, it is a sensation which bribes your heart and the polygamy mindset of a man to fall in a girl's hands who will show the ethic of a love life to him.

Also, love is not being in a relationship like some people who hold on in that just because they are together for years and they won't go apart in their ways only considering the society. It's just a magic. It must lure from the heart towards your girl.

That's the way a couple should remain strong and loved.

She caught him looking at her face without having the soup. She loved that soup at all. More than that she never missed a chance to be with him. Girls won't always look for assets, they prefer best heart ever.

"Have it. What are you looking at?" She asked him.

"My future.... Darling." He replied.

She smiled as she knew how much he was towards her affection. He loved her a lot. Even he was so focused to admire her velvet feather earrings on her ears.

"So, you love this place. Thank god I didn't made a mistake." John said with a relief.

"Hey, can you describe me in one word?" He asked Sumi.

Sumi stopped drinking her soup and kept her spoon aside. She joined her hands and massaged her fingers. He sensed the smile on her lips.

"Do I have to say something, which you know already?" She threw the question to him.

"Just, answer me. I love to hear that from you. May I?"

"Mine."

"Sorry, I didn't get it. Pardon."

"I said you are mine. Do you know how much I cried before when you flirted with other girls? But I loved you very much and see what we are now. We are love puppies. Fingers Crossed."

She did a victory action with her fingers and he cheered for minutes. Behind her naughtiness, there existed a sweet lovely girl.

Waiter came back with the pizza and they had it for the evening. He opened the door for her and she liked his habit of a man as a girl. She waited at the door as he paid the bill and came.

"So, it was a great evening with my loved one." He said as he put his hand around her waist and walked closely. He loved the softness of her skin. It was so smooth and very soft. She made his innocence rot.

She booked a cab as she always did. They sat on his car and talked about how simply a year went by in their relationship without them knowing. She exchanged her anger towards him often with the peck he gave on her cheeks. They both loved each other's company very much.

In the meantime, he called his dad and told about Sumi. He was happy for him as he stood steady in his career taking good care of his concerns and in his life too.

"Welcome to our family my sweet Daughter-in-law cum daughter. John told about you pretty much as you never could imagine. But all he told was with a line, she is my bestie. I smelled something fishy and I am happy for you people to be together," John's dad said her in phone call.

"Papa, as you had told, I must be your beloved daughter. It's my promise I love you and all like how I love John. Without him, am not complete." She expressed her love towards John and his family.

Families are not only responsibilities. They are bonded up with unwritten give and take methods between the members of the family. They love, they scold, they care, they yell but they never want you to get buried. Because you are a part of family.

"I agreed with you to join your family. But you shouldn't tell me to leave my job," she said imperative to John.

"No problem sweetheart. It's your own craze and do it good. By the way, I like the Wild Life Photographer in you."

"Sure, if you are free this weekend, take me to Vedanthaangal. The season is awesome and my DSLR will be loaded with pics of birds."

"My pleasure," he replied. The cab came and she walked towards it.

"Sumi, Just a moment."

"Bro, wait for a minute, I will be back," she told to the driver and she went towards John. In the light of parking area, her face looked so pretty like a constant lightning.

"I'll miss you Sumi. I need a hug," he opened his arms and waited for her to join him.

With a tenderness, she came near to him and hugged him. She hugged even more tighter as she liked to rest her on his shoulder and loved the passion towards him.

"Wow. You smell great, Sumi. It's Yardley Lavender. Smells good on you." He winked with a smile.

She gave a fake punch in his cheekbones.

"You culprit, how do you know these all stuffs man?" She questioned him with a slight jealous in her words.

"Don't you remember, I sat behind Aparna in college days and she smelled the same."

"Just go and die, you devil," she walked away from him.

She rushed towards her and stood in front of her

"I said I like it. But nothing can beat your feminine odor darling."

Within a second, she admired his craziness and pinched his cheeks.

"For our love Anniversary, my small gift for you babe," he handed over a small parcel to her.

She opened it and it was Nina Ricci perfume. He waved bye and she left.

Workaholic

It rained heavily as Abhinav parked his bike in the basement of the IT Park and went to his office. He removed his jerkin and put it on the table to make it dry.

That week was really hectic as the customer needed to deliver the deliverables as soon as possible, but it was impossible.

"It has been three years since you started working here Abhinav. You know all the process happening here. But this time we are really blown. Customer is not happy with the thing we delivered. They will have it and they need another version of it. They insist us to make a new prototype for its alternative. And this would be in their hands in two weeks. Plan accordingly and make your team work for that too. Or else we would get hit badly." His manager made his words clear and accurate.

Abhinav moved along on foot to the pantry and took a cup of coffee. He sat at a corner and thought about how the past week gone and how horrible the next two weeks would be.

"Are you lost in something, Abhinav?" Achu asked as she sat next to him.

Abhinav managed to raise his head up. She patted on his back. After listening all that manager said to Abhinav, she rolled her eyes dull.

She took her coffee and returned with some masala biscuits.

"Saw your time sheet. You have worked for about 63 hours this week. It may increase in next two weeks too. Congrats!! Mr. Workaholic," she teased him.

Achu joined one and half years after Abhinav. Both were well attached. Meanwhile, they were more than friends. She was a keen observer of society and its looks. Despite of changing for it, she preferred to stay as she was always. Abhinav mentored her during her hard times when she was a trainee and she always looked Abhinav as a bro of her.

"That's not a worry Achu. I haven't talked well with my parents and Deepthi. I told Deepthi that I can take her out tomorrow. But even it is Sunday am having work this week. That's what I think about," Abhinav replied with a disappointed tone.

"Wait a minute. Let me check for the booking in Mayajaal. You can go for night shows. By the way which film you want me to book?"

"Two states. She wanted to see it badly. It has been already a week passed since it got released."

"Mm... ok. Tickets are available for 11.45 pm show Abhinav. But not tomorrow. It's for today. Inform her."

"Ok Achu. You can come with us too. She liked you very much from the first meet with her." Abhinav said with a happy tone.

"Aahaan. You couple will watch the movie with a bit more romantic than that. What will I do? Watching that and get jealous."

"Shut up Achu. She doesn't know about my feelings and all." Abhinav shut her mouth with his hand and she removed it with a small bite.

"Go and propose her dude. She will except it." She pranked him.

"F1,F2. Corner seats booked with cheese popcorns and two Pepsi," said Achu.

The clock struck eight. Abhinav went to grab a lemon tea and returned to his cubicle. His phone buzzed. 'Amma' the text came on the screen. He took the call.

"Hi dear. How are you today? Did you reach home or stuck up in traffic?" She asked Abhinav without knowing he was at office.

"Ma, am in Tulsi Park Restaurant. Came to have dinner. What about you and dad ma?"

"He is still in his office. He'll come by late night. Said he will come with some rotis and butter chicken masala. You love it, right? We miss you a lot. Come home soon in this month," she expressed her feel.

"Sure ma, I'll try. Somewhat hectic here. Will let you know ma," he replied.

"Mmm. Take care dear. Go and visit Deepthi. Convey my regards to her," Abhinav gave a positive delight as he was going to meet her.

"It is a weekend, Sunday. So, take rest and feel well for Monday."

"Ok ma. Take care of you and Appa," he said and cut the call.

"Good way of balancing all, Abhinav." His colleague praised him. Abhinav gave a dull look to him.

Deepthi arrived Mayajaal at 11.30 and waited for Abhinav. Abhinav reached there in next ten minutes. Hearing his breathe she understood how he ran to reach here from office. He managed to balance everything a lot and spending time with Deepthi. She loved him from internally, but she never tried to expose it to him.

It was not a fear, it was not a fear of dejection, it was not a fear of proposing. But she thought the time should do its work.

They sat on their seats. Deepthi grabbed the popcorn and had enough she needed. Abhinav loved the movie too.

"Are you into romance genre Deepthi?"

After a few seconds, "Not only romance Abhinav. I like historical fiction too."

"When is our next meet then? Next Sunday?"

Listening to him "We are going to our hometown in two weeks. So, I think I can visit your home. I'll manage to stay in my friend's home at Tirunelveli. As, our family shifted to our native after my schooling, I love to see Tirunelveli desperately and more than that I love to see your parents," Deepthi added.

At morning 6.25 am they reached Tirunelveli. Abhinav got an auto and it went to the way where Deepthi's former classmate Shoba's residence. He left her there and departed to his home.

Wolfie came towards him with his tail wagging for him. Wolfie was a cute Pomeranian dog, who was a dear pet of his dad. He lowered his body to take him in his hands.

Wolfie licked all over his face as they both missed each other a lot. Abhinav's mom greeted him and kissed in his head. His father took his bag and hugged him as the whole family missed him.

In few minutes, he took a bath and returned. After a month of time he tasted his mom's hand-made recipe Fish curry and Dosas.

Nearly after five hours he brought Deepthi to home. She wore a blue silk saree with green blouse and a couple of gold bangles in each hand. She walked like a swan and looked extremely gorgeous on that day. Abhinav's Mom hugged her and she got blessings from her. They met before, but that was the first time she visited their home.

Wolfie wagged his tail and followed Deepthi with Abhinav. They sat in the living room and talked about Abhinav, Deepthi, John and Sumi and the bond between them.

Abhinav took her to his room. She saw his cricket tournament trophies and delighted for his performances.

"Hey, did you study in St.John's School? It's very near to Rose Mary School."

"Hmm. We used to visit your school often for your school girls." He smiled.

She knew Abhinav was just a gem, who respects feelings and differencing it from urges.

Everybody loved Deepthi's company even Wolfie too.

Chicken Curry and Rice with Chicken fry was served by Abhinav's mom. A fulfilled lunch brought an ultimate happiness with his family.

Deepthi saw Sarah's picture hanging on the wall. Abhinav touched it fondly as he missed her a lot and badly.

"We took these pic two days before she was admitted in the hospital."

"She looks so cute Abhinav."

"Every kid is cute and beautiful Deepthi. She was some more but no more now."

Abhinav let Deepthi to see Sarah's drawings with crayons and color pencils. He saved it like a treasure.

"Abhinav, I'll make my move. It's almost eight and dark outside. Shoba's mom will look for me if I am late."

Abhinav started his bike with Deepthi. His parents bid goodbye to her. Abhinav came back to home and went to his room. He missed his most loved one Sarah long days before. But he never wanted to miss Deepthi in his life. He knew Deepthi was in his heart and she was filled everywhere inside him. He just wanted to express everything to her. Time is really dangerous; it won't be with our side always.

Soaring Souls

That night was a big day for Abhinav. "You deserve it Mr. Workaholic" Achu whispered in his ears. She had a tandoori non-veg platter for that evening with Abhinav. He waited for Deepthi's arrival. He put on his trendy black full sleeve party shirt and blue denims for the day.

He called and invited Deepthi over there a week before and he reminded her the last day too. A small party was held for the project success and an acknowledgement of Abhinav's and his team effort in that. Abhinav's manager took the mic and started talking about him and his dedication. Abhinav was expecting Deepthi with eagerness, as he wanted to share the happiness with him.

The grand hall of Hotel RainTree was glittered by disco lightings and a great variety of buffet dishes.

"Where is Deepthi? The program will start in another twenty minutes. Did you ping her?" Achu asked Abhinav, chewing the chicken manchurian.

"Mmm ya. She was started and held up in traffic. She will reach soon."

"Did you bring the bracelet which we have chosen for Deepthi? She will definitely love it. Break everything and pour your love words at all today."

"I am nervous and I don't know how she will take it."

"Godddd.... Every woman deserves a man like you dear. You never know how great you are."

"I don't want to be great. I just want to be with her ever, until I close my eyes forever and my heart stops beating."

"Then it's up to you. As it is your personal things I won't stimulate anything in between you two. You have to take care and my help won't be for you now," she said with her hands crossed.

Abhinav with Achu bought a bracelet for Deepthi two days before from Kanishk Jewelery. With a beautiful diamond centerpiece in the middle, it looked so pretty in its gold color with a lot of design works around it. Abhinav took that as she would love it a lot and had a mind to propose her.

Deepthi reached the hotel. She was dressed in an aqua blue saree. With a mesmerizing peacock designed picture on, it admired a lot of people gathered there. She had a pair of matching earrings and a pair of gold anklet on her legs. Her blouse was in little orange color. She had a simple pair of sandals and she had a lot of stone works in her pallu.

Achu was the one who saw her first and walked her to the celebration area. He introduced her to Abhinav's manager as a good friend of him from college days. Abhinav gave a smile as she returned back with the same. She came near him and did a handshake and wished him congratulations.

He liked it very much. Achu brought a glass of welcome drink and sea food soup as starters for Deepthi. Deepthi had the welcome drink and kept the soup aside.

Abhinav achieved the 'VIBGYOR' performer of the concern for that quarter. The party was for him and his team. Deepthi wished him always to achieve a lot and he never missed it.

The party was started after sometime. 'Jigar ka tukda' with some other top Bollywood songs were mixed and played by the DJ over the corner. Achu had Vodka and Deepthi chose Strawberry Mojito. Achu moved her head for the beats and music of the songs as alcohol drove her mind rocking.

Abhinav looked at her. She was flawless and gorgeous in a simple saree wear as some people spent thousands to have a makeup for that night. She had a little face powder with a small lining of mascara and a shiny orange lipstick which looked juicy on her lips.

With a cute dimple over her cheeks she smiled every time. Everything suited with her pale lemonish skin. Deepthi was not an angel or anything, what stories say about a girl. She was just a girl next door, who ensures your attention on her within seconds on your first sight.

Deepthi exchanged glances with him. Her face turned enthusiastic to dance with him. She came near to him and stood near him. Achu started to dance and she rocked the floor in minutes and returned back to stall for some time.

She held Abhinav's hands and dragged him to the dancing area. She put his left hand on her shoulder and joined their right hand. She looked deeply into his eyes. Abhinav was lost in that and fighting for back into senses.

Deepthi knocked his mind out with the beauty and the expressions she made. As he lost in the eyes of Deepthi, he wanted it to be continued forever.

Deepthi felt the same from the time she reached the party. She was amused to see how handsome he was in the black shirt with blue denims. She had a thought of buying a grey coat for him, which would look so adorable on him. Falling in a man's handsomeness, is not so easier for girl's eyes. But she fell so easily every time, only with Abhinav.

People can dream about their dream boy/dream girl a lot. But one can never get them easily unless the time, situations and even some more factors stop influencing it. Abhinav got Deepthi and she got him. They were made for each other and bonded with friendship for a long time. All they do was caring for each other every time and express the love indirectly on each other.

Loss occurs mostly when we neglect to take a step forward to get what we desired, fearing of the reasons, which leads us to lose that desired one.

Achu wanted him to express his feelings on Deepthi then itself. Even Deepthi was prepared to propose him from the day she had feelings on him. But they stayed as they were. They didn't want to lose each other for the sake of love and stayed to continue as friends. Abhinav and Deepthi were tightly coupled by the slogan 'Best Friends.'

"Reached home safely? Thanks for the beautiful time with you today," Abhinav sent a text to Deepthi.

"Yes, I have reached.My pleasure. And am always happy to meet you every time," she added a smiling emoji and replied back.

"By the way, everyone admired your look today. Somebody said it as my ears heard that often."

'Say that somebody as you Abhinav.' She wanted to hear that desperately. Abhinav loved her unconditionally and was expecting a best time to express that.

"Great. You looked so handsome Abhinav. Trim the beard you have like Robert Downey Jr."

A smile came over his lips, when he read the text sent by Deepthi. He opened his mail and started composing.

To the love of my life,

As I sit here and think about you and what you and I have been through, I see that I can only love you more and more with each day enormously. With every second passing every time, my dreams and my pillow knows how my sleep is lost and you are ruling me in my dreams too. You are my inspiration each and everyday. You are what keeps me going when I just want to give up. You are my reason for living.

When you came to my home that day, it looked prettier by your presence. My parents love you a lot and they asked me constantly do I love you. I denied their question with a lie of just friends. How can I say them that am in love with you from my side only unless I know how you feel. I love the way you show the kindness towards me. I want to love every kiss and touch from you. I wouldn't know where to turn if I didn't have you. You are this boy's dream, which he needs to come true.

I wish you could feel all the passion and all the love that I carry around for you. You have won my heart and soul. You have won it all. From the day, I know about love and sex, I never distinguish it to be with different people. It should be the one soul mate, who should attain all my love and care, my manliness and everything in my life. I want to share myself with my soul mate up to my death.

You make me feel like I am in heaven, in the arms of an angel. You and I have a fulfilling relationship, but as it goes on, I wonder which is it?? Friends or Lovers?? That is specific not yet. We've been friends for four long years now, but this friendship isn't just that anymore, at least for me. I have fallen in love with you and I need to tell you that I am your soul mate masquerading as a good friend.

I must have expressed all this to you, when the college fight was over, but you got that panic attack again and you were weak. I never wanted to gain your attention or gain your sympathy and impression for saving you from that bastard. Love is not that. Love should come from our souls not by the help we did. It's a human thing what I did on that day. You might think me as a good friend and your bestie. Even I think the same, my feelings for you grow more and more, day by day.

Will I get the same from you? Or will I lose you from my life forever if I express this all to you? I think I can keep masquerading as a good friend till our last breath. I can lose my love, but any cost I won't lose you from my life. My heart wants us to be soulmates.

But my brain says 'Let's stay as friends'. What should I do? Will I click pictures on your wedding, with the other guy whom you don't deserve but marry? Will I be alive at that moment? May be physically I guess. I can erase the feelings on you, but Memories... they are eternal.

- your Abhinav

He looked at the message for some time. Without sending it, he saved it in drafts and switched off his laptop.

In Love with You

"Sir, I need leave for 3 days with next weekend Saturday and Sunday. I have planned to go for Goa as a small trip with my friends," Abhinav requested his manager.

"Abhinav, you know the critical situation here. We are in the bad time now. The IT firm is losing its consistency and its projects heavily. And we are in a situation to make our customers too comfortable and satisfied with us. However, we are good in that, I need we have to move good with our business for some time until our side get free little bit. So, kindly don't except long leaves for some months," His manager nicely denied his request.

Abhinav came out from his office for a break and made a conference call with John, Sumi and Deepthi.

Sumi started first. "Please don't say as usual like your leave approval is denied."

"It is. Sorry to say this, but this is the situation here. I can't come with you people." Abhinav said in a low voice as he was sad to lose a good trip.

"It's ok Machan. I understand it. I have talked with Mr. RangaRajan, he assured that he will refer for you in his client's concerns," John consoled Abhinav.

"I know you people will kill me too. My father called me to our hometown. Some function is arranged with his close people I think. I have to go for there in this weekend and will return on next week," Deepthi said to all.

"Sumi, I think we are going for a honeymoon even we haven't planned about our marriage still," John giggled.

"Oho… So, you are having that thought. Let's cancel the plan," Sumi kidded him.

"Oh! my goddess. I will be good. Let's pack for five days. Am counting the days for our trip."

They finished the call and Abhinav went back to his cubicle to do the testing in balance.

"Shower me with Beer and Vodkas. Say No to water," Sumi seated in her seat and whispered to John.

"Ok Madam ji."

"If you give water when we are thirsty, I'll chop your balls and put it to dogs." She giggled so hard and John joined her too in her sense of humor.

They were at IndiGo flight from Chennai to Goa. John booked a room for them at KenilWorth Beach Resort which had the Spa within it.

After two hours of travel they reached Goa. Abhinav booked a cab to reach their hotel destination.

"I have to convince my dad to build a hotel come resort here. It must be good to earn some good money." John thought about that.

Sumi unpacked their dresses and kept in wardrobe. John fell on the bed and went for a quick nap. Within the meantime, Sumi took a bath and came back. Sitting in front of the dressing table, she dressed her hair in a fashion mode.

John woke up in few minutes and saw Sumi at the dressing table.

"I missed a chance, damn! Men should be cautious always." He gave a disappointed look.

"Do I take only a single bath daily?" Sumi smiled and threw a towel on him as he went into the bathroom to take a bath.

John booked a car to go for sight-seeing. Both jumped into it and reached the Aguada fort.

The fort is situated at a hill and its lighthouse is a well preserved Portugese Fort standing in Goa, India.

They stood at the top floor of the fort and clicked pictures with the background of Arabian Sea. Sumi posed sexy-funny poses for John. She laughed often and John loved her a lot.

John drove to Bon Appetit, Candolim for lunch. Sumi saw the pics from DSLR and John gave a small peck on her lips. She smiled and returned back. They ordered Tandoori Naans and Mutton Rogan Gosh.

"Add two French Onion Soups and Fish Fillet with Chips and Salad. Make soups comes soon," Sumi added to the order as the waiter was about to leave.

"You look hot in this orange top with short blue jeans trousers." John complimented her and got up slightly to see her cleavage.

She knew John's intentions and leaned over the chair with her back and put her hands to the back of the chair. She laughed naughty.

Within a few minutes of time the waiter returned with soups. She loved the taste and so did he.

"Deepthi is having a crush on Abhinav I guess. I know Deepthi very well. She likes his company all time as a friend, but now-a-days they are closer than we love couple," She winked.

"Abhinav is suffering badly by the stress from his office. To reduce that I arranged this vacation, but still he couldn't make it," John added to it.

"Mm. I understand honey. You are so sweet," She leaned towards to him and he licked her lips lightly with his tongue.

"Gotcha... There you are - you naughty man. Hey!! They are having Whiskeys. See the menu. Waiter, we need a couple of Antiquity Blue."

Deepthi was at her native, Nagercoil. Whole of her family were attending Mr. Mahendran, The Legal advisor of their community's family function.

"Where are you? How is your family?"

"They are doing well Abhinav. I tried to visit your home in this holiday. But being busy with the function stuffs here. The bride's dad is a close friend of my father."

"No problem Deepthi. By the way, come back as soon as possible. I want to meet you soon."

"Sure Abhinav. Make a plan for a day outing. At least we can go for Pondicherry. You are bit tired with the working stuffs. You will feel refreshed."

"Ya Deepthi, talked with John and Sumi. They are enjoying well and they clicked some pics of Aguada Fort and they sent it. Will forward it to our group."

"Great. My pleasure. See you Abhinav. Gonna Miss you..." Deepthi smiled thinking about Abhinav.

Post lunch John and Sumi were at Dolphin ride in a boat at the banks of Arabian beach near Aguada Fort and left to the hotel room to take rest. Sumi planned to put some tattoo on her back above the waist. John drove to the Calangute Beach at the evening.

"What picture did you make?"

"Will Show you at the night" She whispered seductively.

A great bash celebration was just over. It was just their first day at Goa, but they enjoyed a lot. From Aguada fort to Bon Appetit and then to Calangute Beach.

Dressed in a little white tank top with a yellow trouser up to knee, she pulled John's mad senses out. With the increasing desire for her, he constantly looked at the butterfly tattoo with a lips picture near to it... Well placed above the right of her waist it looked to hot in the eyes of John.

With steer in a hand he touched it softly as Sumi was busy with her doughnut.

"Ssshh… Baby its paining a little."

"Sorry babe. How long it will take to be good."

"He told the wound will heal in twenty days. But the wound deserves a kiss." She giggled as he tried to kiss it from his seat and failed. He put the car near a tree and they both walked towards the Calangute Beach.

It was already eleven at night and the beach was crowded well. They sat for dinner and ordered Pomfret fish stuffed and some grilled chicken lollipops.

"The breeze is nice. I love it darling," John took a piece of the fish and fed her. She loved the kindness he showed on her. John inhaled some Hookah with the food.

"See some bar over there. I need some vodka. Finish the dinner and take me there honey."

They ordered Golden Fry Prawns for the finishing and left to the bar.

Back at Nagercoil, Deepthi was restless, missing Abhinav. She wanted to see him, hug him, kiss him everywhere in his face and tell him that she loves him the most than anyone in her life.

To the man of my smile and blush,

Gentleman, this princess here is waiting for you to grab her and fly to our kingdom. I wanna make coffee for you daily morning, and prepare everything for you for the whole day. Keeping you happy every night and the day. Feeling the love with you every second. I hope I will express my love on you coming Friday evening, when would meet. The moment you said that you miss me was the time I felt how we need each-other's company.

Are you a wizard? What magic you have done on me? It may be an old film dialogue but it won't stop me from saying it. You made me feel how a man should be for a girl, the kindness you showed, the care you gave, honestly am very lucky to have such a friend like you in my life.

Do we still need the blanket like 'Best Friends' circle? I want us to step ahead and be closer more than we are. I never saw a man taking care of a woman in her periods like you when I had and out of meds. Love won't happen just by flirting or sexting honey, it must lure from both hearts independent of Estrogens and Testosterones. When two souls combine, what could stop them? Religion? Status? Caste? Nothing.... I say nothing. I never looked for anything than you sweetheart. You are the one I need ultimately. I know the way you will take care of me.

Finally, the day I close my eyes to sleep forever, I will be seeing you. Wait until Friday, I will make a surprise proposal for you.

your Ravishing Bae.

Deep Inside 'U'

The trip was going so good for John and Sumi. They have visited Basillica of Bom Jesus, Our Lady of Immaculate Conception and Panjim on mornings. After morning, they went to Arambol Beach, Miramar Beach and Dona Paula for the evenings. For nights, they rocked with their feet at Casino Royale at Panjim lake banks, Paradise Boat for discos and Primrose for DJ night.

Sumi enjoyed the trip awesome with her beloved one. She was always in his arms, as she gave a small peck on his cheeks and lips between hours. John felt lucky as he couldn't find a hot and lovely girl throughout his life like Sumi.

"I need some massage at Spa. But we are away from our hotel," she was annoyed.

"Mmm… Let me Google for it. We might not get Star hotel Spa benefits here. I can make local people massage parlors for you honey," John said as he surfed for massage parlors in Panjim.

They parked their car near a Vada pav shop. Sumi got down from the car and put her coolers on. She came back with two Vadapavs with delicious tomato chutney. She had a bite and gave another to John.

"Got some. Think they are charging very cheaper than our hotel people. So, that we can tip them good."

Sumi nodded in response to him.

"Hi, this is John calling from Panjim. We are two tourists here. And we need some Thai massage and oil massage on the back. Are they available?"

"Hello Sir ji. Yes, yes... Its available with us. By the way what kind of people you need to do massage?" A guy on the other side asked John.

"Mm... We need two people who should be proficient professional in massage. As I saw that you are charging 4000 for an hour. So, we need two hours of it with the steam bath available there."

"Sure Sir, as you preferred we will provide our good services. We are having individual rooms for that too. You can enjoy the pleasure and we are the best one to provide excellent service."

"Oho...ya, I saw it on the internet. Most of the people preferred and rated you well with good comments. That's why I called you. By the way can you list the services you people can do for two hours?" John asked the massage guy.

"Hey Darling. Its hot outside. Let's sit inside the car and talk," Sumi pulled him inside and he continued the talk.

The massage guy listed his services, "Sir, for an hour we will do a great Thai massage by our two Russian professionals. After that if you want them the girls can continue. Or else we can choose some of our Indian girls to service you.

They will continue the service with oil massage for forty-five minutes and Happy Ending for fifteen minutes. Your pleasure is our satisfaction sir. You will never forget our service sir. As you said you are in Panjim, you can reach our place in twenty minutes of drive."

He finished his list and let John to speak. John had a mild doubt by the word "happy ending" and put his phone in loud speaker so that Sumi can hear too.

"Buddy, I didn't get you. Did you say "happy ending?"

"Yes sir. You are right."

"What does that Happy Ending include?"

"Sir, the masseur will do the massage being naked. You can touch, feel and taste them as much you tip them. But Happy Ending is included from the massage cost and they'll do oral fun service for you."

"Oh.... Gosh... I will call you," John cut the call as his heart beat furiously. He never heard about these stuffs and he started sweating by that.

Sumi looked him silently. Within few seconds she was burst into laughter. She couldn't control it and she got out from the car and ROFL leaning on a tree. She teased him with how he was feared and what panic he went through. She realized John wasn't the old one, who was towards girls and their stuffs. He was treated by the love of Sumi.

"So, do you need the Happy Ending?" she giggled and asked him.

He shook his head hard as she again had a great laugh. He drove to the hotel in some minutes of drive and went to the Spa there with Sumi. Taking a small nap, they left to Calangute Beach for their final night of that trip at Goa.

John opted Souza Lobo for dinner. John put on his Black Hoodie T-shirt and Camouflage ¾ 's for bottoms. Sumi chose blue partywear gown, with some floral works near belly. She looked stunning when she walked towards him as she tied her hair like a Green Trends model with the Black shiny shoes on her feet.

John came into senses and pulled her near him. Walked into the hotel they grabbed a pair of seats.

"Two glasses of Ciroc Red Berry Vodka first with a plate of Butter Fried Squids," Sumi gave the order.

"Add a plate of Mixed Seafood Grill and Crumb Fried Chicken with that too. Vodka and Squids should come fast," John said to the waiter.

Waiter left the place, taking the order. John took Sumi's fingers in his hands. She touched it slowly with a passion for her. She admired the way of his touch and how sensitive it was when a loved & deserved one play with it.

Sumi took a sip of Vodka and made a 'Wow' reflex by its taste. John fed her with Squids. Having it a lot, she enjoyed its taste with Vodka.

"Four golden days Sumi. It won't get erased from my memory. My love is growing more day by day for you, I love to be with you all time. You are a boon, dear honey. After your photography session in Bengal next year, I'll talk to my Dad to make our wedding arrangements."

"I talked with my parents too, they accepted my decision as they are broad-minded," She said in response to him and nodded his statement.

They finished the dinner and went for a walk at the beach. Sumi stood near to the Sea as she fondled the amour with the Sea breeze and Tidal sounds.

John stood back of her leaning on her body a little grabbing her hips in his hands. She cherished every moment, she was with John. For John, she gave the meaning of love and a complete life ethics.

"Baby, let me try some tequila shots over there," Sumi requested John. And he accepted it with a smile. She pinched his trimmed cheek and walked towards the stall. John followed her.

As usual, the Calangute Beach was in the rocking mood, with a hot music of Sunny's special 'Pink Lips'. People dinning and the couples dancing, had filled their hearts with intense ecstasy. John ordered two shots of Don Julio Tequila.

"I saw in a tutorial, like how to have it. Follow me," she said with a little proud of joy in her eyes.

"Remember to lick, sip, suck. These are the basic steps to have tequila," John winked.

"I know sweetheart. Am a pro by the way," she winked back and poured some salt on the back of her hand below the index finger.

As she licked the salt off her hand, the salt lessened the burn of the tequila. She drank a shot in a single gulp. John giggled by her enthusiasm on it. She took a lemon piece and bite it quickly. She sucked the lime on its wedge.

"Feels good and drugged," she laughed.

"Lemon felt good for the burning taste of tequila. Wanna try some?" she asked John.

Without a denial, he took it and gulped it immediately. He went near her. Putting his right arm around her waist and grabbing it tighter, she pretended to be unaware of that. She wanted to tease him a lot.

Without giving a choice for that, he pulled her forward towards him, he turned her to face him. She could see the burning desire for her in his eyes. With a lot of love, he looked directly into her eyes, joining fingers with hers.

Besides the beauty of that early night, the full moon showered all the light over the beach. She looked dazzling with a light makeup on her face. Her skin looked like a firing flame. It was so shining and looked so smooth, which killed the innocence inside John. Sounds of tides were cool and they sensed the moisture of the air.

Sumi pushed him away and walked towards the table. John followed her and gave a little spank on her back. Loved that from inside, her look made him feel so special that night. She had a couple of tequila shots and started dancing again. John was in no mood to waste that wonderful moment.

On Looking her skin dazzled great in the light of the moon, he turned uncontrollable. Her waxed legs were so great that and he didn't miss to gaze.

They looked at each other, felt the jolt in their eyes. She smiled seductively as his mood aroused a lot. Immersed in her beauty, he didn't want to waste the time. John stood right back of her and gently pushed her hair other side and kissed the back of her neck a little.

Leaned towards her, he rested his chin on her bare shoulder.

"Honey, I think we can play some intense games in our place right now."

"So, it's just games right. There would be nothing other than that tonight," she giggled.

"Honestly, there are plenty of games left. Want to try everything with you this night."

"You'll be out of games and its ideas in upcoming times and night," she teased him heavily.

"Do you know, before every game, a warm up session is important too," she added naughtily and winked at him.

While she was up to another tequila shot, John took her laid in his arms. Started walking to their room, she was enthusiastic for every next seconds of their life. She put her arms over his shoulders and sensed the extreme love in his eyes.

He rolled her on the bed and went top on her. He kissed her forehead and cupped his cheeks. She looked deeply into his eyes. Loving him a lot, she trusted him firmly.

"I am not on pills. Can we go for a protection?" she whispered in his cars.

"Ya, we should have. Ok, take a bath and wait, I will be back in minutes." He gave a peck on her lips and went.

Sumi remove her gown and tied a long towel on her. Walked into the bathroom, she thought of how important was that night for them. She cleaned herself well and put on his favorite 'Nina Ricci' perfume. She wore a beautiful white saree with georgette works on it. With a nice zebra patterned velvet blouse.

As she entered the bedroom, she dropped her jaw in surprise.

A velvety black one piece up to knees with a pair of red lacy inners were placed on it. A pair of floral designed long black stockings with a perfect black coffee blend color added there too. She saw a paper at the middle of the bed having the text *"Wear me!"*

With the purple and red rose petals he decorated the bed so erotic. Two dozen of candles and a small diamond shaped gold bulb was lit. At last she found a red colored eye mask at the corner of the bed.

She dropped her wearing and slipped into the outfit he kept for her. She rolled the stockings on her legs, which looked so voluptuous. To add a little spice tonight, she applied some eye exotic eye shadow bought two days before. Finally, she put on the eye mask and waited for her prince to fulfill his intentions.

John opened the bedroom door from the hall and sneaked in silently. He never saw his love goddess so sexy and beautiful before. She was sparkled in the black outfit with a set of its matching shiny black stockings and sitting like an innocent baby lamb on the bed with eye covered.

Like a typical man he gave a scan top-to-bottom. Thinking about ruling the night, he slowly unbuttoned his shirt. With all his love towards her, he leaned towards her with his. She let her hot breath out strongly, as she was expecting an unconditional play.

Love always comes with no conditions. She felt the smell of his masculine aroma and enjoyed it. He took her chin in his hands and planted a kiss on his lips softly. On feeling the softness and moisture of her lips, he tasted the top and bottom lip alternatively. Sumi tilted her head a little, made a way to hold his head by her hands.

Turning too passionate he pressed his lips deeply with hers, she explored every nook of his mouth with her tongue. She was so voluptuous and had an 'Am all yours' feel towards him. John slid his tongue inside her too to taste the sweetness of her kiss ride.

His hands went to her eyes and removed eye mask. He went to her ears and started tasting it. She felt the hotness inside her ears, as he gave all his breathe inside it. He licked it passionately.

"Happy fourth year Love Anniversary," she whispered in his ears in the sense of being at paradise.

John cupped her cheeks, "You are the best thing happened in my life."

He continued the kiss as he placed his right hand on her breast. He felt the softness on his hands and turned horned by her comfort with him.

"Ssh. Stop my horny idiot," she pushed him to the bed.

"Don't you want to make love?" he asked with confusion by her reaction. She ran her fingers on his face and teased him.

"I mean, help me to get out of this hot wear, to show you some valuable things in this planet."

"Ah... That's a coolest way… Sorry. That way must be too hot. May I try to handle that?" he grinned.

She sat turning back towards him, as he unzipped her dress from her back. She slipped it to the floor and his lips moved onto the back of her neck slowly. Ventured even lower, he was losing his control. He wanted her so badly as she was determined to have it too.

Enjoying the sensation, she kissed again and again on his lips. Being enjoyed it a lot, he did a reflex back it well all the time. From a beginner to veteran, they were trained well within few minutes of their kissing session. John could feel the sexual tension between them. Their kiss was more passionate every time. She fell on him facing his bare chest by her face. She ran her face on it.

"You look so beautiful and sexy in this," he said pointing her top inner garment. She took his hand and placed it on her right asset.

"Feel me and taste me Darling," she looked straight into his eyes, started removing his jeans. He came closer to her and turned her back towards him. His trimmed beard, went up and down on her neck to the underarms.

He loved her feminine odour combined with the smell of the perfume, which drove his mood a lot and made him sense horny. She felt his saliva's moisture via her sweet sweat.

"What's Next!!??" she asked with a great eagerness. He turned her back towards him.

"I didn't expect it from my hot guy,"she made him comfort with her and gave every nook of her for him. He started showering kisses below her neck to covering the neck behind the ear. With a great pleasure and sensible touches, she moaned in pleasure.

He bit the strap of her inner garment and pulled it down. Taking in his hands, he threw it away. She was delighted for the next move and looked shining with the small drops of sweat on her spine. He moved his fingers all over her back. She felt the ticklish sense with pleasure.

He licked her neck, as he felt the softness of her neck. She rolled facing towards him and bit his lower lip demanding some more.

He played well with her lovely assets and went to her belly. His tongue danced and licked her curvy hip and belly as she held his head for the support to handle the pleasure.

John made her wet, not her eyes. She caught his sensible nerve point and made him even horny. He glanced at her body as she blushed much for the first time. She looked so cute and hot after her face. He held her hour glass and went down for her. She could feel the intensity of his lips and the air seemed to be growing warmer.

"I love it… Do me good as like now...." she let her words out with the immense sensations she was attaining. He was appreciated good by her words. On kissing her lips, he slid his fingers softly so that she could enjoy a lot.

"Let's do this. I can't wait anymore," he whispered in her eyes and turned off the lights.

In the lustrous mixture of candle lights and the gold colored exotic light, she looked illuminated and shining. They deserved that night and didn't want to waste a single second. One thing lead to another, they mastered like a pro.

Lovemaking is not only feeling your partner physically, it's for understanding what she/he needs and loves to get from you.

He paused for some time before positioning him towards her. He kissed her so deeply as he loved her most than any other in his life. She was the one for him and he was one for her too. They felt more comfortable in each other's arms than being alone.

She held the arm of the wooden cot as he admired her beauty inch by inch completely.

"Shall I?"

"Go on my prince, rule your own kingdom. Do gentle... It's my first time."

"For me too."

John opened a pack of protection and rolled it over him. Sliding him inside, she let a drop of her tear, he felt the initial pain she felt. He kissed her eye and tasted it. Men are not only lusty, they are sentimental a lot too. He felt him inside in a velvety zone. She loved being with him and making love with him. He pushed himself slowly and steadily with deep strokes. She let huge breathes out every time as he buried his face between her cute assets in pleasure. She moaned heavily, as she felt the pleasure flowing towards her spine from toe to the head. She bit his shoulders in the mild pain she felt every time with pleasure.

Pushing himself in, he cared about her a lot. He held her hour glass in his arms, and grabbed it steadily. Seeing the pleasure in her eyes, he felt loved every time. The love aroma was spread inside the room under the erotic light with some dozens of candles brightness, with two souls exploring each other physically and more mentally for the first time. Sumi took care of his sweat gland. She made him sweat so hard as he worked on her a lot.

Real men won't need Viagra to make love with his soul mate for every time, it's all of mere and immortal love he gets and delivers to his partner. It lures the pleasure of lovemaking and the passion of love on each other.

Sumi went loud exploding a huge breath out as she reached the climax. John slowed his pace and moved slowly into her. She hugged him tightly as she felt it for the first time.

Orgasms are not only for the end, it can be a start for the next one too. He held her waist and rolled her back. He looked the tattoo with the kiss image with the butterfly below her spine clearly.

"You are extremely longing to see it right. It was shown in a perfect time," she said in a romantic voice.

He kissed it and put himself in, laying on the back of her. She loved the passion he had always with her during the session. She felt him every time so good, and his manliness keeping her pleasurable with taking care of her.

After a few insides and outsides, he felt came. With a moan in her ears, he felt his climax.

He laid next to her, with his arms covered her waist and belly. She buried her face in his chest as he felt the softness of her skin. More than everything they loved the way they love each other.

Most of the times, the lust is also too pure to express the purity of love.

They were not only love puppies and they marked more than that in each other's heart. Estrogens and Testosterones were overridden by the kindness and care for their love.

That was their last and perfect night for the trip in Goa. Not only feeling their assets, they felt themselves mentally and physically stable with each other which would be forever.

In love, the intimacy & care is marked always as 'should be' and 'must be'. There would be nothing so called 'may be' and 'will be'.

The Stare She Gave

Deepthi returned to her senses. Abhinav called her and remembered their meet on that day at Forum Vijaya Mall. Even she was expecting that from him, she was too meticulous. Not only meticulous, she had already stored a lot of pain inside her without letting him to know how immeasurable love she had for him.

She grabbed a white Chinese collar top and a grey long skirt for their meet up. She put a pair of red stone studs on her ears. She looked herself once again and prepared for the meet. Her mind was already in a state to explode all the love on him. Words never ever work out, but the feel must. One can be proficient in words, but words can never express what the vibes they are going through.

Thinking about you always, I want to make it to the end zone,

What to do I just stuck and beaten in the friend zone.

The pretend zone,

Where I walk cautiously to be close with you, thinking about being closer.

Love came with no warning,

Lost myself in its flow.

Know everything is alright,

Kneeling down towards you during your sight.

Pretending like everything's alright,

Am cheating myself a lot.

Walking around the circles,

In the darkest nights,

To explore what I have for you....

I have to know,

What you are having for me first,

Because am ' Friend-zoned '.

Abhinav took a corner seat at the McDonalds restaurant. He wore a purple full sleeve shirt, tucked in with a shiny grey pant. His Woodlands denim shoes added a neat elegance to his outfit. Deepthi sent a text to him that she would be half an hour late, because her dad messaged her to talk with him immediately.

But his soul was unstable. His mind roamed everywhere like a bee to the sweetness of his life and bitter side of it too. He knew past is past, but he always cherishedthe thought about Deepthi and the wonderful days with her up to then.

It was the day he was going to express everything to her. From love he to life he would make for her, he prepared everything to be expressed. Deepthi parked her Vespa in basement. Taking a lift, she came ground floor and walked towards him. With her cute smile on her lips and a soft dimple on her cheeks, she melted him a lot.

"Classic cutie Deepthi..." he thought as she started ruling his mind with her charm already.

"Dude, sorry for being late. Dad called, so I had to stick to the call for twenty mins."

"No problem. It's my pleasure to meet this madam, a busy bee after a week."

"Oh shut up… Some program is being organized there. Come, let's see," she grabbed his hand by her palm and pulled him to follow her. He imagined that moment for long that she would hold his arms while he walked, a dream come true. But at that time, he felt happier, he never knew that it was love or magic. Simply, he loved to feel that sensation.

They reached the center free area of the Forum mall, surrounded by the stores in various floors. Love-Guru program was conducted by a FM channel as they took a seat opposite to each other. Deepthi ordered two Banana Milkshakes.

"So, what's important today? In four years you never said that you missed me like you said two days before. What's going on in your mind?"

She let him answer. Making him say some words from, she gave a chance for him to play a Romeo Role.

"Mmmm. Let me guess. Hey, Did you get a date? Finally, you found a companion for you right," she said after a couple of minutes of guessing and started to tease him.

"Yes Deepthi. I am in love," Deepthi tilted her head and looked into his eyes. Abhinav saw her eyes and tried connecting with the sparkles it emitted.

"I know her from our 12th Grade. The day I saw her, I was lost in her since then. Years went and days passed by, but my love towards her hadn't changed a little bit. Despite of everything, I focus only on her presence with me and the love I was about to shower on her for life time," he was interrupted by Deepthi.

"Is she coming here now?" With a shaking voice she asked him. She never expected this bombshell from him. Deepthi cursed herself for her madness of being late. But what to do, he loved her since he was seventeen.

Do you know how it feels, when your loved one speaks about his/her loved ones? Getting stalked by your own shadow in the ways of dark forests and stabbing yourself by the agony you are going through.

Deepthi felt the same at that time. She never thought a girl would come and save Abhinav from her. Behind her tears in her heart, she has always faced him with the smile.

"She is here Deepthi. She'll be here in few minutes."

"Oh... It wouldn't be pleasant as am being here like a pillar for two of you. I will take my leave now."

She dropped some tears as she turned her face away from him. He held her hand and asked her to sit on the chair. She turned her face again and swept the tears in her eyes.

Bringing the smile back, she made herself comfort there. She made her mind to see anything now. Better she should be prepared, that's what came into her mind. Letting someone to grab your soul mate, whom you deserve is the biggest lose you will attain if you do.

He came closer, "Deepthi, I have prepared to express my feelings for her. May I impart it to you? Just for a preparation dear buddy. Promise," he added.

"It this what you give for me dear God? Hearing all the words he is going to pour from his heart to his deserved one. And I am sitting like a dumb ass, showing nothing in my face and wishing them. It is not cruelty my dear Creator, you made me scatter simply by just a smart move. Congrats dude! High-five," she looked towards the ceiling above meters from her.

"Ok I'm ready!!" She said as she came back to her senses with some moisture on the corner of her eyes.

'If I could be anything,

Dear Honey, I would be your tear. Sorry to say this, but I wish I could be your tear, so I could be born in your eye, in your flesh, flow down your cheeks and die on your lips, as you taste me finally in the next life.'

She said whatever came to her mind, but everything in life has a full stop. It determines the place you have to be as you are. It came already for her. She stopped in her right place without uttering anything above.

Both of them stayed silent as they were never aware of each other's presence in their souls deeply.

Love is always unconditional, it shouldn't be handled, until you both loves to surrender themselves to it, without thinking about its consequences. Apart from love, two souls have to be trustworthy, honest and the have magic feel for each other.

"I never felt nervous like this Deepthi. With you I'm very much comfortable to face anyone or anything."

"Thanks Abhinav. Make your mind for her, Start!"

She made him to be focused and let her know what he was going through. She opened her eyes widely, inches away from him, hands crossed, looking into his eyes firmly, noticing his body mannerism, she listened everything.

He held her right hand and rubbed the back of her hand. She understood he was nervous and he did it for a support. As a friend she never let him cry on pillows and on college desks. Both of them were pretty in the heart and supported each other whenever they were in agony or the hardness they went through, or whatever the life offered to them.

"It may be little bit surprising for you and may be you won't believe what your ears are going to hear. Honestly, withcourage, I really want to deliver what I feel and what I sense: the magic whenever I'm with you.

From the moment I saw you, I felt a connection between your souland mine. I desired for you and waited everyday on the path of your footsteps, the way you walk towards your school. I can still remember exactly how you looked the day I first saw you.

Your beautiful smile captured my heart and your cute smile over your lips with a cutest dimple I ever saw erased any and all doubt that I had ever thought about a woman and her beauty.

Even in that usual Chudidhar, you were deadly gorgeous, with a small amount of jasmine flowers on your head, with a little bit on your lips, when you admired the cuteness of the sparrows on the wall nearby you. I am sure it was your usual day, but it wasn't one for me.

When I told you about Sarah and I was sad, you opened your arms and hugged me. It was the time I felt how important you are in my life. One should console and share the pain what we are going through. But none should come with us for the life to share it all and everything.

The kindness you showed towards me and my family mesmerized me a lot. My parents were asking about us? What could I say? Just we were friends. Caught and stuck up in friend-zoned. I never want to say that baby. I want to live with you. I know you are the 'home', right where I had always belonged.

I won't forget the day you took me to the temple. It will remain embedded in my memory forever. You know the exact words to put me at ease and the time when your hand reached out to hold mine, while entering the temple, I realized that I had found my future, my soul mate and the love of my life that I had always dreamed of discovering before. May be I am seeing the longing, the passion, the truth in your eyes that you want me in your life. But I am really weak in figuring out ever.

No woman was closer and lovable to me like you next to my Mom. When she said, you are the girl whom they loved to make a family with me, I felt rejoiced, but I kept smiling with a sentence 'We are friends.' I didn't have an answer when they asked me 'Why don't the better friends be better halves in life?'

We talked for hours about the subjects which were the trendof the day and stopped to look at each other when we fell short of words.

I am sure whenever I see your eyes looting your heart secrets, your dark secrets, it was the reflection of the same incredibly intense desire sense that I was feeling. The time we sat next to each other, was the time the whole world had ceased to stop. The only thing that beat in our heartswas the emotion we kept for each other.

My joy would be more intense, richer and deeper if I get heard from you the words I dream of all the day. The moments when we were apart, when you were in your hometown, seemed like a bitter eternity and you never know how barely I waited for you to see you today.

You must be the only person, who can cause my heart to skip a beat with just a side along glance which you gave multiple times at the temple the other day or a gentle smile, with the dimple where I had fallen a long ago. Every time I gaze into your eyes, I lose myself and I forget where I am or what I am.

Ever since the day you came into my life I have known what true love and desire really are, the emotions that many will never know in their life time. I want myself to be not your option, I want myself to be your priority all the day and nights, being with you. I want nothing more than spending my life with you always at your side.

When I wake in the morning, I want to find you always beside me. Whenever I go to sleep at night I want to feel your arms holding me and hugging me, with the warmth of your body. You are the only true love of my life. I never felt this before and couldn't with anyone in future.

I Love You, my dear Darling. No matter what our future holds for us, I will love you even I couldn't get the same from you, until the end of my time in this planet.

I say it again 'I Love you, my babe. I am madly in love with you."

Deepthi was in confusion to whom he was confessing everything. She looked aroundto find who the lucky girl was but all she could she was nothing than some people watching the event.

She doubted that it might be herself. On the other hand, she made up her mind that she didn't deserve it. She held his hand, pulling him towards her,

"Dude, where is she? In the above floors?"

Abhinav saw the nervousness in her eyes and words. She understood the thing he loved for. She urged him to say what she wanted to hear. Abhinav sat silently, as he admired the loveliness he felt on her face.

'Mr/Mrs/The Creator, are you going to make me to believe, you are existing? Definitely not. Because, you might have created humans, not angels. ' He smiled as she threw her hands in air of his void answers.

Abhinav got up from his chair "Stay here, don't look back." Saying that in her ears, he went two chairs back from them. Returning with a basket of roses and blossoms in his hand, he stood like a kid giving a gift to his friend for a birthday. She smiled at him for how romantic he was towards his girl.

'Dear god, she is lucky' she felt inside.

He took the bracelet which bought for her on other day, and placed it in the middle of the flower petals. She touched the petals and felt the softness with the more softy one, her hands. She admired greatly about the centerpiece on the bracelet.

"How sweet you are! A girl must need this kind of proposal. She must be lucky. Lucky to be in your hands. And I'll beat you after sometime to confess about her after a long time." Abhinav looked so adorable. He charmed greatly from the day she saw him. It is hard to find a guy like him with the genuineness he had and the honest he was towards all. She felt that from him, but never saw such a romantic idiot in him.

"When you are going to say and express this all to her?" she asked innocently.

"I did."

"When? You idiot buddy?"

"I love you Deepthi. That's what all I want to express to you."

She stood stunned, with no response. Deepthi didn't shown any reaction, he expected. Instead of that she stayed there like a statue. Abhinav ran to the crowd, few meters away from them. He grabbed the microphone from the anchor and came towards her.

None of them noticed what happened there before. But then all eyes were on them.

"To the love of my life." He took her right hand in his and put the bracelet slowly on her hand. With a loud applause the crowd was seeing the most romantic segment of the evening in the mall.

Deepthi turned her hand and stood silent, without knowing what the reply she could give.

He took a hand of roses, stood in his knees. "The day I met you was the day I made my mind for you. You are the spring of my life. Without you, am incomplete. The other day, if I'll be in the knees in front of a girl, it must be only to tie the shoe laces of our daughter. I am someone else when I'm with you. Someone more like myself."

She sat on the chair, removed the bracelet from her hand and kept it back in between the roses. With tears on her eyes, she came towards him. She rubbed his hair fondly, cupped his head in her hands and kissed his forehead.

"I am not the girl you deserve. It's not for me. It's unwritten," she smiled with the tears, turned back and walked towards the gate.

With the crowd, he stood there in his knees down on the ground, with the love stream in his heart, with the agony he was feeling. After a long stare, she went missing from his eyes, but definitely not from his heart.

To the man of my blush and smile,

You might move on from this, just like all who doesn't live with whom they love a lot. You will fall in love again with a new girl you'll see in a coffee shop on a rainy day in near future.

By the way, that might lighten up your life. It may make you forget the time you loved me. But, that are all my Abhinav can't do. That's the problem my dear, that's the issue with this cute adorable man of my dreams.

For the past five days I was restless, thinking of you, the ways I missed you every minute. Even when I was prepared to say you everything earlier today evening, I made my mind how can I impress you. I know you won't expect any impression from me but I did all.

Love is like a war dear, it's very easy to begin with but really hard to stop. I don't want to put you in the situation like this, so what happened there was the decision I took it for. The time I prepared myself for the arrival at the mall, my dad called me and conveyed me that he promised my marriage with his dearest friend Mr. Mahendran's Son Ranjith. He said a lot about him bla bla bla, like he's a construction engineer in Mumbai and all. But none went into my ears, when you are inside my veins and blood always. What can this poor girl do, when fate presses her with its iron feet. And when you said you love someone, I was worried as much as delighted for a life with other girl. But when you said it is me, I lost in my dreams and the world I always lock myself whenever I think about how we will love in future in my dream land.

Nobody is worth my tears when you proposed me and I stood dumb without having a mind to accept it. Do you know how ironic it was? I went through a great agony. The time you talked about our daughter in future, it was that much hard to avoid my thoughts to hug you and say the love by lips on yours.

So, what should I do now? Burying all my desires in myself as I ever do. Or will I express it all after saying about you to my family.

Life is like a Tsunami my Romeo, it won't come easily and it won't remain anything.

With tears, Your Ravishing Bae.

She went to the kitchen and took a cup of buttermilk. She thought how his passion might tear into pieces. Tears flooded from her eyes. She closed herself in a blanket. Only her pillow knew, how much it rained on that night.

Hate Me Once, Love Me Twice

Abhinav had a break from his five hours sleep. Despite of living his lovable life, he indulged in much more work stress for the past one week to reduce the pain of the denial. In her perception, he didn't have any anger or suffering by Deepthi. He cared all about, her presence with him, which could be changed for this reason.

Deepthi called him, to go for Aasife Biriyani for the weekend evening. Going for hometown, he sent the text. Both weren't close like before, but dying to be. He stood up from the chair he slept and walked towards the pantry.

Switched on the TV, having a Horlicks malt, he thought about his good olden days. The days which was so pleasant to be an unknown admirer of her. She never came to know in the months he followed her closely and betrayed his studies.

With a serious heartbreak, he suffered a lot. Took some pills to get some sleep, but that was not he deserve. No medicine in the world is fair enough like the care given by our loved one.

You are the girl I saw from my heart,

You are the girl I desired to live for decades.

You are the one who gave me all the best time in my life,

Finally, you are the one who dragged this all from me.

No matter what happens,

I will never change myself,

You know I won't change how I feel about you.

Deepthi wasn't voluptuous, she was not the girl of every boy's fantasies. But she had something more which every guy in this planet deserve most. Got birth in superior family of her native, she came out through it and showed love to all the human she knew and saw. She never showed the luxury and all whenever it followed her too. That's what a girl should be. As per her name, she lighted the lives of some kids by funding seventy percent of her salary as a Probationary officer to the kids who were suffered from various syndromes and HIV.

Despite of looking the figure and the assets of a girl like a typical boy would want, Abhinav never did any cheap things. More and more he was very protective with her and loved the path they were.

She missed their conversations a lot.

"My work will finish at 6.30 pm. May I wait for you at Kumarakom Restaurant for evening snacks together?"

"I can't be there today. Going to show the demo with clients. It will happen up to late night today."

"At least get some sleep. Heard you are working double the time daily. If you feel insomnia, let me take you to a doctor."

"Am not an insomniac, am just a workaholic."

"I know what you are than others. Be safe and healthy. Call me when you are free."

"Sure". He took a corner seat in the pantry, avoiding the vision by the cameras. When he was with her every time, he never tried to be happy, it just happened all time.

Abhinav swiped his mobile screen, as he went through the pics of Deepthi with John and Sumi, when they went for the last trip to Pondicherry.

' I can find a prettier girl than you, smarter than you and funnier than you, but I will never find a girl just like you, Deepthi. The love of my life. Seven years and how could it be screwed up soon? .' His mind was flooded with millions of thoughts. But everything was marked with the name Deepthi.

Back in Deepthi's place Sumi came to their flat and jumped to the ceiling to the floor to tell things about Goa. Deepthi was too happy for her. He kissed her cheek as Sumi giggled with the kindness she shown.

Friends are not only well-wishers, they are the ones who will bring the well, satisfied, happy life towards you by the love they give. They didn't know that God did all these or any others, they only thing which drove them all was the friendship they had. Sumi took her hands in hers and sit nearer to her. She gave a neat white box. With lot of curiosity, Deepthi opened it.

"For our friendship my sweetheart."

It was an orange banarasi saree with lot of stone works in the jacket cloth with a stunning finishing in the border. With the golden blouse cloth, it looked extremely good. Deepthi wasexcited when she saw that. Sumi kissed her forehead. The love they shown to each other was like sisters. They came from different wombs, but nothing separated them.

"Do you know? Abhinav got selected in X-Code Developers Ltd, which is an UK based Indian firm having four branches in India including Chennai. Just now Achu pinged me on Whatsapp. She tried to catch him up, but he departed to his hometown soon today. He will be the Associate Architect there," Sumi expressed with a glance in her eyes.

Deepthi was too happy for her. Moreover, the pain she gave for him pained her a lot. Some people are being in love for a reason, some deserve but stay away for another reason. She was not good when her father fixed her life with the guy he knew, whom Deepthi didn't had a look at all.

Parents are too possessive in India. They choose how they should grow, what medium they should study, what department they should take, what course they should do, what job they should get.

Finally, for the sake of being their child, they reserve the rights to decide who shall be their soulmate.They never see what their child likes. That is a selfish mindset even. With some care, it always happens to have their honor. That's what Indian society lives and fucks everyone's lives.

"We all like him; he is an exact guy for you. He is getting a handsome salary and they accepted your love with the profession until you became pregnant." Deepthi's mom said nicely in phone call.

"Ma, but I don't even know him. How can Appa fix this?"

"Deepthi, you are not in an age to decide your future. You are just a chotu with a lack of life experience. And this alliance is from his dearest friend's family from our community." she added.

"I can't decide this so soon ma."

"See that's what I told too. You can't decide all these in this small age. Let it in our hands, we elder know what is good for you."

"Ma, I said I can't decide this so soon. Don't try to make me believe am a kid. I am twenty-three and I'm independent," she made her point clear.

"I can't argue with you as far as you are not convinced. Have in mind Deepthi, you should be traditional and calm. You are a girl "

"I'm also a girl.I know what is right and what is wrong for me, more than you ma, I'll choose my life good and fair. Don't try to forcethe family's decision even on my marriage. I know better who can I live with peacefully. I can't live with someone I have never known or someone I don't love," she said strong.

"We are visiting you with Ranjith this Sunday. He liked you very much from the pics he saw."

' Damn, how can these men decide just by the looks. Think fair skin is a good price in this marriage market? What about my feelings?'

She felt it disgusting. Even in her hot conversation with her mom, Abhinav came plenty of times in her mind. There were plenty of scribbled thoughts about him in her senses, she scribbled his name hundred times in the diary, with her name preceding his.

'Hate me once for my denial, Love me Twice for the love I will show.'

Bleeding From the Heart

"Deepthi, our DP taken in Goa got 450 hits. See how we were in the front of Sunset at Dona Paulo," Sumi turned her laptop and showed it to Deepthi. With a pale orange sky their image in the pic looked great.

"What about your next trip? Where are you planned to go?" Deepthi asked Sumi.

"Mmm. I have planned to take John for a surprise trip to Kerala. You know boat houses right. It would be fun. But I postponed it for four months."

"Kerala. The place of nature. Sounds cool."

"You are having sore eyes. Did you sleep yesterday or not?"

'I haven't slept good for days dear. ' Deepthi thought.

"Am going to have a Skype call with my bro Rajveer and will be back in an hour. Order some lunch for us in Foodpanda," Sumi finished and went to the other room to have the call.

Deepthi went to the thinking about the reactions which might arrive if she revealed about her affair with Abhinav to her parents.

Every time she thought about that, plenty of things came into her mind. From A to B she saw many positive love stories with a great negative end. As she thought about it, she knew the lovers were lost, the love didn't.

"I will take that for you Amma, how are the people in our native?" She went to the bus stand without any intimation to talk with her parents before Sunday.

"They are all fine Deepthi. Everyone asked about you. Most of them cared about you. Some of their words are of jealous for the job you are having and the salary you are getting."

"That doesn't matter for me, Ma."

"But Deepthi, leave your job before marriage, that would be a keen move of a good girl yet to be a bride."

"Stop that ma, I must remain as a good girl not a girl dependent on others. I know you and dad made me. But this is different than that. I have answered your next question before you gonna ask me," She made her look straight and delivered her statement.

"She grown up in city. We have to tell about our native cultures," Her dad added with her mom.

Deepthi booked an Uber to drop her parents at their hotel room in SaidaPet. The app showed the driver is seven minutes behind of their location. She thought this seven alone minutes were enough to convey it to her parents.

"Ma, I shaped my marriage life and my future with some expectations in my mind and dreams."

"Don't worry a lot, did we see a simple guy for you? He is a well settled, good earning one. That's why we said you to quit your job. He is going to take a project in QATAR soon, so he said that we can make marriage preparations next year."

"I didn't come to say about the money expectations. Stop that nonsense first. Money is not only the life. Apart from that there are much more"

"I know my dear. But the much other you specified mostly comes under money. It has the will to buy anything."

"Bridge between souls, stands on pillars of trust! It reflects united self and creates a path to reach each other's hearts. You never understand this. Money can't buy these three: Happiness, Trust and Love."

Stopping her mom, she continued.

"I love a guy who is my best friend from college days. He protected me and cared me in many ways that I haven't seen a man did that all to a girl in my life."

Deepthi's mom stood upset with her daughter's words. Before considering the happiness and love her child would get from her loved one, what came up into her mind was 'their people' their 'community people.' Caste is a stinky useless shit, used to stir the unity among this society. It fucks our lives easily with a simple word 'Caste Name.'

"What is his Caste? And are you really out of your mind? How can our family face our relatives and the society?"

"He is a respectable man and a kind hearted human than all of us. He saved my life and my soul. I love him and I never leave him at any cost."

"For your information he is also same as our caste. So, ignore your thoughts and do what can make your daughter happy. If you still consider what relatives and society talk about, kindly think that your daughter of your caste is dead," Deepthi added.

A slap came from nowhere to her cheeks. She rubbed her cheek with her right hand as she felt the senses of pain through her nerves.

"Never repeat this again. Did we grow you up to see you are dead? " Deepthi's mom yelled at her. At the same time, the Uber taxi came near to them. Deepthi left them in the car and took her bike to her hostel.

When people fail in love, unsaid thing stay unsaid forever and stay with themselves. But the people crave for their love, fight with the society to earn the love they made up to a marriage have the things to say each other up to the end of their lives.

Within the four walled, closed room Abhinav laid on the bare floor with the hoodie T-shirt and jeans pant on. He kept a small pillow for a support to his head. The moments with Deepthi in this same home came into his mind. With her presence the whole house was rejoiced. The pillow sensed his sad mood and caught his tears on it.

Abhinav showed the same amount of love to him, even more than Deepthi sometimes. He pulled a bed sheet near and put it near to Abhinav. With a wagging tail, he licked his face with a lot of love towards him. Wolfie put a hand around him and slept near to him in his pillow.

They two shared their love on each other every time they see in a month. Some are undefined. The love between a man and dog is a great bond in this universe.

He heard a beep tone in his phone. He saw Wolfie is sleeping, he put his phone in silent mode. Abhinav stood up and washed his face, opened the Whatsapp message box, he saw the one from Deepthi.

Deepthi: Hey, how is your family and you dear Wolfie?

Abhinav: Ya they are good. They have left to buy some groceries.

Deepthi: Bring some gulab jamuns prepared by aunty. I love it

Abhinav: You don't have to say. My mom already made it ready.

Deepthi: Can you come to Chennai tomorrow?

Abhinav: Anything important?

Deepthi: Not important. But it would be nice if you are with me tomorrow.

Abhinav: Oh, its Sunday right. I forgot. You will go for Hanuman temple.

Sure, I'll book a bus and will reach tomorrow.

Deepthi: It's not for the temple. We have to talk about us.

Abhinav: Mm. Ok. Time & Place?

Deepthi: Usual. Starbucks, Pheonix Market City.

Abhinav: Hmm. I'll be there. Bye. Take care.

Deepthi: See you Bye. :)

Abhinav didn't understand what she wanted to say. "Let's stay friends, that's what she is going to instruct me" he thought.

He drove his bike on the Tirunelveli – Kanyakumari Highway. The wind from the sea shore to the lands hit on his face as breeze. He sensed the moisture in the air. From 75 kilometres apart from Tirunelveli, Rastha Kaadu is present in the left side of the highway. He parked his bike under a coconut tree's shadow and walked towards the beach

Covered by the trees on the both left and right sides, the way showed the path to the loveliest sea shore before Kanyakumari. Apart from three 10 years' kids no one was there. They played with the tides on the shore and enjoyed the noon time with the water.

Abhinav sat there still with the thoughts of Deepthi. He could live without her. But the way he looked her every time, he dreamed about the life he was going to have with her in future. She didn't give answer to him like not a handsome one, not good guy, not a man, not a human of kindness, not showing respect towards woman and all. Because he knew about him and much more than that Deepthi knew about him a lot.

She never said the reason, she left him barely in tension and the pain of denial with no reason.

Achu visited the nearby town for her college mate's marriage. She pinged Abhinav to know where he was. She stopped at the famous halwai shop in Tirunelveli and went to Abhinav's home. She found that his mom and dad were only present in the house.

She called Abhinav and got to know he was in the Rastha Kaadu Beach and she drove the car to there. In a devastated bad mood Abhinav stood there like a corpse. She consoled him and took him to the Bang's restaurant. She never knew him proposed her and the answer was a denial.

She made him to say the story from the start of their life and he did. From the school days to up to now, they crossed many pages of their own beautiful life pages.

"May I talk to Deepthi? She must have a strong reason dude. Deepthi is not a girl to reject a guy for no reason."

"Who said there is no reason Achu? There must be one. We are not aware of that. Someone's lucky than me Achu. Or else I didn't deserve Deepthi by the writings that Mr. God did as you people say ever."

"Ok. Ok. Stay calm my dude. Life is not what it does with you, life is what you make and what you can do with that in the rest of your days."

"Advise is easy Achu. You can never understand how much agony am going through."

There was a deep silence between them. He never looked at her face.

"Sorry, I shouldn't have told like that."

"If next time a sorry comes from your face. The teeth count of your mouth would be reduced to thirty-one."

She winked at him and hugged him.

The Words for You

Deepthi made her mind to accept his proposal on the day he proposed her. But time played well and the situation ruined all. She waited to let her family know about her love first before him and she did. She never knew before she would fall in love. Whatever comes to our life, if we are steady and confident, we remain as we are.

"Packed gulab jamuns in the box dear, Give it to Deepthi tomorrow."

"Seri ma, you are so sweet."

"Do you like her?"

"Who don't like her ma?"

"Don't play with the words Abhinav. It's your life and you are the man to decide. If you do, let her know soon."

He kept silent and packed his things. Wolfie assisted him to the gate. He bent towards him. Wolfie licked his neck and face and put his hands on his shoulders. Love is eternal, it doesn't depend on creatures.

"Take care of my Girl," His mother waved her hand with a bye.

He turned and smiled her.

Being in love is like falling into a beautiful blissful sleep. It happens slowly, then very suddenly you find yourself asleep. You then find yourself never wanting to wake up again. Falling for you dear was not just like that. I still don't want to wake up and I hope that I never have to. I hope with all my heart that this is reality. I hope that you are not a dream, but that you are the girl of my dreams in real life. I hope you do not fade away, but that you stay with me forever. I love to be your man, holding you, loving you, having you forever. I love to melt in your hands every seconds of my life in the presence with you. Living in the hope of that Deepthi.

Deepthi sat with her mom and dad in Starbucks coffee shop, Pheonix Market City. Her parents were really not into this love kind of things, so they felt disgusting by their daughter's decision. But Deepthi sat calm and excited to meet Abhinav after long days. The girl who loves passionately has no other thoughts in her mind than her man.

Abhinav opened the door and walked in. He wore a neat casual combo of blue check shirt and black jeans. Deepthi waved and he noticed.

"By the way, this is Abhinav." Deepthi introduced him to her parents. Abhinav sat opposite to her.

"We are friends from the first year of our college and he is my bestie. Working in a software concern, he does his job as a Team Lead with a handsome salary. A handsome man with great qualities," She added.

Her mom never raised her head up and simply sat there stirring her coffee. Her father who was in Safari suit, looked with anger in his eyes towards him.

"She is saying much and praising a lot uncle, I am just a simple man of my mid-twenties."

Deepthi's father punched his own thigh and got up from his chair. Taking the handbag in her shoulders, her mom followed him too.

"See this guy standing here Ma and Dad. He is the guy I love. In fact, he is the guy am going to live my whole life with. Bless us and accept the way we are ma," She held her mom's hand and told with a daughterly love towards her mom but she left like unnoticed.

Abhinav came near to her and looked straight into her eyes.

"They are just considering some useless stuffs more than our pure love Abhinav," She said in tears flowing from her eyes towards cheeks. He rubbed her cheeks and made it dry.

"I love you Deepthi. A good marriage is the union of our marriage soon," He smiled.

She took his hand in her palm and smiled twice. She again giggled. She blushed a lot too. He opened his arms, eyes closed and welcoming her. She gazed at his chest and fell on it. She pressed her face on his chest and she hugged him.

"It's enough. People are watching Deepthi," She hugged him even more tighter.

"I know I hurt you a lot, when I denied your proposal just like that."

"It only hurt me that day because I expressed you my everything when I had nothing to let my words out. That's was the feeling, Deepthi."

"I thought that my boyfriend loves me a lot and he knows it," She winked.

"Yep, even I tried to hit on Achu," He teased her.

"Aahaan. Then what's this unshaved beard stands for. Don't say it as style. Damn, it looks dull. Go and have a good look."

When one person can fix your heart perfectly, other person can shatter it into million pieces too. That's what happened into Deepthi's life stream too.

Back in the hotel room, the argument between her and her mom was furious. Her mom was stiff and strong in her voice. She never wanted a guy out of her religion. Even sometimes she mentioned that Deepthi was a kid and she was like a puppy in a dangerous man's hands. Deepthi ignored that all and showed her trueness in love. Her dad sat silent in a chair of the dining table calmly.

"I am your mom, Deepthi. Right or wrong, we parents' will show you the path. How can you trust blindly a man whom you know for few years only?"

"He saved my life and my body ma. Moreover, that I love to live a good life with him. What stops you allowing me for him? Caste... Society? My foot. It's all shit that screws people's life. I don't want to be a victim like the past lovers who gave up and lived a fake life for all these beliefs," She made her point strong.

Her Dad's phone rang. "Hey Mahendran. We are in Chennai. I think I have to come for Nagercoil and talk with you in person. Deepthi is not well to meet Ranjith tomorrow. So we can make it few days later," He cut the call and packed their belongings.

"Appa, Don't be silent like this. It kills me. Do you still think your caste is more important to you or your daughter?"

"Yes it is Deepthi. It is an honour to be a man of our caste. Ask your mom, hear the answer you will get from her too. It won't change. The pride and honour you will never taste from other things than our caste's own pride and honour."

She broke into pieces. "So, you are saying your daughter is no more."

"I never said. Kindly don't make me say that in future," He lowered his round specs and said her.

With all the tears in her eyes, she pulled her father's hand. "I am most alive, when we are in love," she said straight to him.

"You will understand what is important in the life. No love can make your life happy and blessed, Deepthi, it's all about society, relatives, parents and your own community."

She joined her hands and sighed him to leave. She closed the room and its windows. She sat at a corner on the floor and cried a lot. Surrounded by the tears, she sat there with the sore eyes, and the thoughts of some conversation with her mom and dad.

Someone knocked the door. She stood up and rubbed her eyes with the napkin. The room boy came to clean the floor.

"We have to clean more something important than this. Messy society shit," She left with a crying heart.

Her phone buzzed with the vibration.

Abhinav: Where is my kitty?

Deepthi: Can you come to Saidapet and meet me at the railway Station?

Abhinav: Sure, wait for 10 mins. I am at Alandur Metro.

Deepthi: I need your lap to lay my head and cry. I don't want to shed my tears   on this street.

Abhinav: On the way dear.

They sat on a bench at a park in Saidapet. She laid her head on his shoulders and was silent. He touched her head softly and rubbed ran his fingers into her hair. He understood the agony she felt.

"I am lucky. I get to spend the rest of my life with my best friend who just so happens to be my wife. Love you my chella Kitty," He whispered into her ears. He sensed nothing reciprocated from her.

He kissed on the centre of her head and sensed the smell of her hair. He loved her with the mere honesty and trust. He was a man of ethics and the pro in the meaning of love. She raised her head and bit his ear. She smiled and rested her head again on his shoulders.

"Can we give a shock to John and Sumi?" He winked at her and she did the same to him.

"You lovable idiots. Am I in my dream? Am so happy for you darlings" Sumi shouted in air.

They were at Hotel Tulsi Park, Tnagar next day.

"For another love puppy," John raised his glass filled with a cocktail of lime soda with some grape syrup. Sumi pulled Deepthi and kissed in her cheek. "Happy for you Darling, got a lover to love you more than me," Deepthi giggled as Sumi teased her.

"Today's Night is ours. John, grab tickets for four of us tonight at a disco. Deepthi, baby don't say Mom will scold you." Sumi mocked at her. Everyone laughed with Deepthi.

Biryani was served to them with the fried onion rings on its top for the lunch. Sumi called the waiter for a chicken gravy and a mutton schezwan fry. Abhinav fed Deepthi often with his hand and she loved to get it than from her own hands. They both looked adorable and cute. The best pair had joined. An honest Tamil man and a typical south Tamil girl, tied by the term of love by the love of so called Mr. God.

"I am still scared about my parents. They are in a state that I never saw them before. Is loving a guy without their approval is that wrong?"

"Actually the society where you live in are infested with literate idiots, who favour separations based on religion, caste and superstitious beliefs," John said and picked a piece of chicken with a fork, chewed it.

Deepthi nodded in response. Under the table, Abhinav held her hands and patted on it. She trusted him and he always made that trust strong every time. That's what love and friendship should have.

Relationship lives on reliability of the people whom they are with.

Caste – The Match Maker

Deepthi was at the bank, checking her accounts. It had been a week since she had a talk with her parents. Abhinav was also dug up with his work. Being in his notice period, his company crushed more than the limits until he went out of the office to another one.

Abhinav wanted to meet Deepthi. He pinged Deepthi for that. Deepthi called him gladly after seeing the message. The last message came from him before 32 hours.

Deepthi: Hi gentleman, Whats up?

Abhinav: Just wanted to hear your voice kitty. I am really fed up with this shit work.

Deepthi: It's not new for you, gentleman. Just adjust and compromise for two and half months. Nothing more.

Abhinav: Mm... Let it be on my side. What about your parents? Did they talk to you after that?

Deepthi: Never. They think I am deceiving them and ignoring all their traditions.

Abhinav: May I talk to them?

Deepthi: Lol... My dad and mom never made me feel that sad. They love to do it now. Because of the thing I did it for ourselves.

Abhinav: Just hold on the line. Mom is calling.

Deepthi: Take her into conference.

Abhinav put her on hold and talked to his mom. She showered all the love and care on him.

Abhinav: Amma, wait for few seconds.

He connected the call with Deepthi too. Deepthi and Abhinav's mom was silent.

Deepthi: Hello, Abhinav.

Abhinav: Haan Deepthi, say Greetings to your aunty.

Deepthi was stunned by his act, even his mom too. He continued.

Abhinav: Ma, we are in a relationship, and we want to marry with your wishes. You, can find a girl for me anywhere. But over the 7,162,119,433 girls other than you in this world, she completes me and she is the girl for me.

Mom: Happy for you both. Bring her home soon. Not as a friend, as your fiancée. Deepthi will be my own daughter. God Bless you Deepthi.

His mom cut the call. Deepthi was rejoiced and felt blissful. "Why my family is not sweet as like Abhinav's?" She felt bad about her family.

Abhinav went back to the work and received the mail from Deepthi.

To the man of my smile and blush,

It is so hard to understand that am missing you so much every time when I think of you. We are just sixteen kilometres apart but the thing is you are stressing so hard. Whatever happens, the love I have for you would never reduce. Don't get panic that my parents get me away from you by some emotional blackmails and all. Am I a chicken.... I am Deepthi. The girl of flame. Lol. It sounds funny right. I tried to get some smile on your face dear.

It has been a week I had a talk with my parents. Heard from my cousin that they asked some time from Mahendran not telling our love story and saying like am not ready for the marriage. The craze I lure for you won't fade. I love you and just a smile of me will convey you all. You are the wizard who made me like this, you hunk. Let this kitty be yours always. Have me near you and say some romantic bed time stories.

Eagerly waiting for the day to be yours. To the love of my life.

your Ravishing Bae.

Deepthi was in great anger. Her mom deliberately wanted her to marry the guy they want. She was almost tired of answering their questions for the past two weeks. On the other hand, Abhinav was in his work badly. Last week he wanted to go for a day outing with Deepthi. He felt it might be a relaxing one for both and having a good time together.

When he asked for the weekend Sunday to his manager. He looked him up and down like a body scanner. He rubbed his hands and made a stern look again. On a serious note, he was instructed not to take leave on the Sundays too. He had no option until his notice period gets over.

Within the two weeks, all the emotional blackmails were done. Deepthi was not heartless to just being with Abhinav's side all the time and not caring of her family. She hated the casteism what her family followed. Humans should be seen as humans. Where is humanity when an unneeded caste method ruins the life of crores of people.

The country we live in always wants to know our surname to know what caste category we fall into. We see in some areas that the caste name is included with their name. But that is not the honour you earn for your life. Eternity should be in vision of life and ethics with the kindness and help you give for others, not the vision on caste.

"Leave him and come with us Deepthi. We want you back as our beloved one. You are the entire world for us."

"I love to be with you all ma. The fact how much you people are important to me is the same for him in my heart too. Never think you can overrule what has been written in my mind." Deepthi replied calmly.

With phone on the right hand, she rubbed the tears coming from her eyes.

"I never know this caste and its principles made our people so brainless."- She sent it as a text to Abhinav.

"Let be broadminded and lighten the society which hate the people like us." The reply came.

In the next week too, the same rhymes from her mother was heard. It made Deepthi really irritated.

"At least think about your parents who wants to live with some respect in the society and among our relatives. Do you think you can live alone without us with that stupid guy? He is not a man for you Deepthi."

"Ma. Do you think you are the one who determines everything in my life? It's my life and I have the rights to choose who is best and suitable for me. The criteria list you have is the narrowest one I have ever seen."

"Is that only your life? Just have a good answer... It's ours. Family... Try to understand, my child. Hope you'll get changed from the stupid decision you have made.

Sari leave that. Are you going to Hanuman Temple often?"

"Why not Mom? I do."

"Thank god. At least you are doing it for our sake."

"Yes often. Because I have no one than Abhinav to yell about the difficulties am having with your madness. That's the reason I visit our God often, Mom."

She cut the phone call and put it back inside her handbag. She patted herself and walked towards the Mehta Sweets. A pair of Gulabjamuns on a glass bowl dipped with jeera came. She took the force and made a sensible cut on the jamun and tasted it slowly. Behind the sweetness of it, the invisible tears of her was hard. It is the hardest one to wipe away so easily.

She gave a don't care talk with her mom, but deep inside it hurt her more. Grown up by a huge family, she was cared a lot. She wasn't able to control the tears that emerged from her eyes. She didn't want to weep in front of all. She took her bowl and seated on the last corner table of the shop. It was raining outside. Looking at the rain drops, she sat there looking it with good focusing.

The rain drops fell with no resistance, like a free lanced software engineer, who works on his needs. She took the cream bottle near her and applied a smiling emoji on her another jamun.

With the moisture on her eyes, it seemed happy by her vision through it to the jamuns.

Problems of India

"You should keep your girl in your finger tip. See what happened. This is what happens when our girls go to City and study nothing about academics but other things," Vasudev said to Deepthi's Father. Vasudev was their community head for their circle. He stood there like a lamppost to all the community problems and was favoured by his people.

"When she overruled your emotional blackmails, she deserves the bad punishments we have in our society. Does she think that the love will be forever with her?" He added and questioned him.

"Yes, Vasudev. She always blabbers that. I have grown her with so much love and care. That's the worst thing one should have done."

"Do you really think that was the thing which created all these problems? She should have known about our caste culture. Broadmindedness is the thing which ruins our kid's mind. Make her understand about that all."

03 - Aug - 2016

Deepthi fell on the ground at the moment her head hit on the wall. Her mom pushed her head right to the concrete wall and Deepthi went motionless. Deepthi's aunt Nithya called the ambulance and rushed her towards the hospital.

Few minutes before that incident, Deepthi's whole family circled her around at her room and started convincing her. It started with just convincing and went with brainwashing and finally it turned brutal. Deepthi hadn't shed any drop of her tear and she stood strong and demanded what she deserved.

Her dad relation aunts cursed her. One of them questioned her 'Did she sleep with Abhinav? '. Deepthi replied with patient and calmness ' That's not what love is. And he is not the man you people have in your mind. He stole my feelings, not my virginity. '

One of her uncle told the example of how they denied their cousin's love and finally made them to marry a girl of their own caste and how he was good in his life with his kids and wife.

"Is that guy mad? That girl chose your cousin as a wrong man." Deepthi thought.

She never ignored her family that much before. Grown up in a love filled family, she was so obedient. When she realized what was the one she needed forever and the path she chose determined her will towards it.

Abhinav and John parked their bike opposite to the side walls of Le Meridian Hotel, Chennai. Walked towards the road side shop they ordered dosas and eggs.

John came back with two plates of food for that evening. Abhinav took a piece of that stuffed it between his teeth and chewed it.

"Indians love to see love marriages in movies. But they won't support them in real. India is a country of romantic movies that doesn't even believe in love marriages." John cursed.

"I haven't got any call from Deepthi still from yesterday. May be she is depressed with her mother's torture," Abhinav told in a sad tone.

"Indian parents have a very good logic dude. We should never talk with strangers. But they fix our marriage with a stranger and they want us to sleep with them on the very first night with our newly unknown married partner. They know love marriages are good, but if they accept it, their dignity and pride will dissolve from the society. What matters them is society, not their child's happiness. Not a little." John gave a sarcastic smile with the end of his statement.

"Bro, another egg for us," John gave a quick order to the shop guy.

"I think of marrying her, John," Abhinav told about his decision.

"Deepthi won't do her marriage with her mom and dad's wish and blessings," John responded.

"She is not only their girl. My mom already said me to bring her daughter home soon," Abhinav gave a smile after he chewed a large part of full boiled egg.

Back in hospital, Deepthi was discharged after four days of treatment. She had a little blood clot on her head, which could be treated with tablets itself. Her mom stayed in her room and was adamant. Her aunt Nithya discharged her from the hospital and cleared the bills before that.

"Still paining dear?" Sumi asked Deepthi with care. She arrived that morning and heard from Deepthi about all the incidents that had happened. Sumi was shocked to hear that a mom had tortured her beloved daughter.

"They won't say they accept, until this culture of having caste based temples all over this country," Deepthi gave her statement good and clear with a smirk.

Sumi rubbed Deepthi's head and she bit her lip due to the pain. Sumi took her for a walk outside. They walked on the platform of the road from ITC grand Chola to Alandur Metro. Sumi talked about her meeting with her brother Rajveer and about his Girlfriend 'Tanu'. She showed her the pics of them and the pics of her with her little lamb. Sumi wanted to make her happy. At least she wanted Deepthi to cheer somewhat.

Amidst of all the happenings, Deepthi remained so silent and she thought about Abhinav all the time. She didn't disclose it to him.

She called Abhinav. Waiting for her call, with the flooding love Abhinav took the call on the second ring.

Deepthi: Hi Gentleman. Miss me?

Abhinav: Baby, Kitty, My gulkand. How are you devil? Why I haven't received any call from you for the past three days.

Deepthi: Nothing gentleman. We had some asset documentation with my family members. So, they all came here. Missed you so much.

Abhinav: I won't say that all. My hugs will make you feel that :). You okay na?

Deepthi: Ya Ya. Everything is good. Your sweet and sour peach is always here with you dear darling.

Abhinav: Behind all your tears, you're are still smiling. Erase that all and light my life.

08 - Aug – 2016

Abhinav felt restless for the last three hours. Deepthi was with him all the time, holding his hands with her. Ended in vain, when he came to know about the brutal incidents held last week from Sumi. Sumi and John decided to say that all to Abhinav and they did.

He never had any anger on Deepthi. Not then too, he was just sick with the things what her parents did.

Is falling in love with the human is that much cruel in India?

Funny our Indian parents are. They will give us all the freedom including everything, but they never allow you to take a decision with your marriage. Elders think, they are experts and professionals in choosing the bride/ groom for their son/daughter. The most idiotic thing is, they even decide when we have to enter into our wedding night room at the auspicious time noted by the astrologer. Like religious atheists they are always not bright in their words. They know how a marriage should be done. The decorations, the invitations. They will do everything pakka. When coming into the region of choosing the partner you are a stranger even for your own partner selection.

Love is volatile, it evaporates directly from the hearts and spread into each other's soul. Deepthi packed up all inside her tightly contained heart. She was never aware how ease it will be out.

Abhinav controlled himself and sat with Deepthi as she rested her head on his shoulder and thinking about their life.

"Deepthi, have you brought your phone?"

"Yes I do. Here it is." She took her mobile out from her handbag.

Abhinav went through her apps. Deepthi was there with no motion simply admiring the looks of Abhinav and how he made her strong with good endurance.

"Booked tickets to Tirunelveli. We are departing tomorrow night. Pack for yourself."

He drove her to her room. Sumi opened the door and hugged Abhinav. Deepthi went inside her room and took her gold Kerala Saree. Packed it inside her bag and pinged Abhinav.

"Bring your ethnicity to our ethnic place."

The single tick turned double with blue color.

Love(r) Bites

"You are a Devil," Sumi said and pushed John away to the lawn. He fell on the grassy lawn and gave a stylish pose towards her. She mocked him like kicking on him as he rolled for a couple of meters away from her.

"Babe. What have I done? Am like a lovely kid. You let me do that…!! Don't blame this innocent kid sweetheart," John replied in a kidding tone.

"Achaa, this baby deserves a kick on his balls," She giggled.

They were at the Guindy National Park. It was already past 6 pm. Couples like John and Sumi had chosen their perfect place and experiencing their romantic sessions. Kids were playing in front of the park. Sumi and John were under the shadow of an old banyan tree.

Security would run them out in nearly half an hour. 30 minutes, that was what they had for that day.

"See my neck, you idiot. It turned red. How can I go to my Art class to teach?" Sumi showed her neck to John and made a cute face.

"Babe, am not the only one responsible for what happened now. I grabbed the indication from you and then..." John said with a gulped smile.

"Then what... Did I ask that?"

"Do I need your words?" He exclaimed mischievously.

Sumi took his hands, let his fingers to move on her tattooed neck. He ran his fingers more up and found the reddish color on her skin.

"Baby, I just wanted to kiss you in the neck. But that tattoo with your desi colored skin turned me on and it made me crazy. You know what happened next. A small little bite gave a small red blush on your pale smooth skin. See even your skin is blushing," John explained to her like a child.

Sumi grabbed his nose with her fingers and whispered.

"You are a Vampire... My idiot partner."

She kissed him on lips and started walking towards the entrance.

"See you at 9 am tomorrow," She added.

She left the place on her Vespa. John started to his apartment thinking about the romance of that evening.

Deepthi stepped her right feat inside her man's house. Wolfie came to invite with his usual tail wagging. Abhinav's mom came to receive them. Kissed on Deepthi's forehead she hugged her. Deepthi got blessings from his mom and dad. His mom showed her room and she rested for a while.

"She looks so broken."

"Her family is torturing her Amma. I don't know how to convince her family," Abhinav told his mom.

His mom was concerned about them a lot.

"Did you talk with her dad and mom?"

"Nope Amma. I had a phone call with her Dad. Leave her, that's what he said." Abhinav replied to her mom.

"Ma, call Appa. I have to talk something with him."

His mom went upstairs and called his Dad. He was reading the newspaper. He placed it on the table and walked down to the living room.

Deepthi got refreshed as Abhinav's mom gave her a cup of coffee to have. She made Deepthi to sit on the Sofa and Deepthi did.

"Appa, I know you gave me all the freedom of my life every time. I know you'll hate if I thank you for all those. You always taught me the love and kindness. I can't see Deepthi getting scolded and beaten brutally all the time. Her mom even cursed her for being a girl of their family. Disgusting talks about her are also getting spread. I love Deepthi from my soul. She is the one who completes me a lot."

He went near her and held her hands. Rubbing it softly he continued.

"I want to put a full stop for all this. She was the most pleasant one, whom I want to spend all my life with her showering all the love on her. My entire life will be adorable with her. Deepthi, the love of my life. John and I would go to meet with her dad and mom tomorrow with each-others family lawyers. Hope it'll go good. Deepthi is the one born for me and I am born for her. :)"

The very next day John arrived to Tirunelveli with his lawyer. Abhinav called Deepthi's dad and he came with their community head Vasudev. Heated conversations went. John and Abhinav stated the points with much patience and meticulous. Vasudev was very fiery and he opposed everything with the thing so called 'Caste'. Deepthi's father joined with him and objected all the words of Abhinav. He even said of filing a complaint against him for kidnapping her daughter.

Abhinav felt this won't be good ever.

"Sir, I never thought in my life, that humans of this caste stupidity exists. My parents raised me with two words - "Help and Care." I live by the way they paved for me. You know how much me and Deepthi love each other and how our life will be. You can look for lakhs of men for her, but you can't get a guy he loves like me. Try to understand that first. Rituals, Prayers, Caste everything was made for our own causes. Don't let them rule us.

I have never loved anyone like her. She is my first one. And she must be my last one too. I could never love anyone else like her. She knows me completely. Apart from all the things you gave to her, she combined with me by the soul. With pure kindness, change your percept from being a casteist to being human."

Abhinav said softly. Deepthi's father looked tensed and angry. He closed his eyes for a moment and in a no time, he slapped Abhinav twice on his cheek. It was a strong slap as it pained Abhinav a lot. John pushed him aside and jumped over the table to give a blow on him. Within the centimetres distance from his fist to Deepthi's father's face, Abhinav stopped. John cleared with his lawyer to take all legal activities if they try to separate Deepthi from Abhinav.

12 – Aug-2016

Achu was at office and received the call from Deepthi. She was delighted to see it. After Abhinav joined the new company, she never got a chance to meet them, because they both were in struggle with Deepthi's parents.

"Hey Deepthi. Darling. What's up? How are you? How is that sweet idiot of yours?" Achu was curious.

"Hi Achu! Everyone is fine sweetheart. I hope you are great there buddy. We are in Tirunelveli, have come to see Abhinav's parents," Deepthi replied Achu.

"Great. You could have informed me too na. I must have come with you."

"Not like ignoring you dear. Problems arose from my side. My parents are very much sticky with their own caste preference. And we both are against that every time. Still my parents are not convinced and my dad slapped my man too. Things are going very bad. Abhinav suggested to be like this until my family get convinced. But I know they won't change. Even if they try to change, my relatives and their caste minded brains won't let them to do."

"So, what's the decision you are planning now?" Achu asked Deepthi.

"Hold on a second. Please say you are getting married to Abhinav," Achu continued with eagerness.

Deepthi gave out a smile. She took a breath.

"Yes, my sweetheart. We are getting married," She said slowly.

Achu jumped from her chair and shouted in happiness. She kissed Deepthi via phone call and expressed her greets.

"Love puppies. Am putting my ticket via Spicejet and coming there. To kill you both with enormous love and kisses. :) You people won't know how much happy I am now," Achu added.

Deepthi said 'Love you ' and cut the call. Abhinav was there smiling towards her. She touched her one strand of hair and put it back behind her ears. She lowered her face due to shyness.

He sat on the sofa, simply watching her walking towards her room.

In Chennai, Sumi and John were at Elliot Beach, Besant Nagar. John parked his BMW near the KFC restaurant and bought two blue Mojitos from Cafe Restaurant. They walked on the platform and then on the sandy beach. Both sat on the sand on the shore of the sea. Waves came and touched their foot often.

Sumi played with her hands running over John's face.

"We write with our heart, not with the inked pens," John said Sumi.

She raised her eyebrow with a little amusement.

"Sir, started saying romantic quotes? Interesting."

"Men are not so expressive. They do good in right times," He winked.

He caressed her hair softly. She dissolved in his eyes and his touch.

"So, when our love puppies are getting married?" She questioned him with mere eagerness.

"May be at the starting of the December. Still three months to go. Pressure is so bad from Deepthi's parents. They can keep her as their daughter only if she agrees for their meaningless statements. I would never be like Abhinav, he is so patient. Even when her father slapped him, he remained silent. I would have slapped him back too. But Abhinav stopped. He is a good human not a caste starved immature thing."

Sumi got from his lap and saw him straight. With a slight amusement, she gave a small smile. John kept staring her. Her kohl and her eye combo was killing him silently. Men will always men in what they do and how they admire. Every man love his girl in his own way and John was not an exception.

He loved Sumi and he was so clear in what he does. She gave a kiss sigh towards him. He was silent like a statue.

"So, if my Dad is also so stiff and strong, not letting me marry you, what will you do?" Sumi asked John.

"You know what I would do, my darling."
"I expected some different answer baby," Sumi gave a disappointed look.

John looked at her. She needed an answer. She needed to know how desperately he was in love with her. Holding her hands, he walked towards the car in the parking lot. Putting the car on ignition, he drove it to the Casaurina Drive.

He stopped near a villa and Sumi stepped out of the car. He pointed the Villa and said her to go in. He felt the joy in her eyes. She opened the gate and walked in. With the sea breeze hitting all the time, the Villa looked so beautiful. It had two floors and a good architectural design with yellow and white colour paints. She walked inside the Villa. A big collage of the most important moments of John with Sumi was on the wall. She kept watching it. She admired all the pictures on that wall. Every picture was a memory.

John stood behind her hugging. She touched his cheek and gave a peck.

"For our love," he whispered in her ears. She kissed him again.

The Wedding Planner

"I'm so happy for you, buddy," Achu came quick and hugged Abhinav tightly. She did a long handshake with him. Abhinav's mom greeted Achu and asked her to sit on the sofa. She offered Achu some native sweets and a cup of coffee.

Deepthi came to the room, after taking a bath. Achu jumped from the sofa and ran towards her with a bright smile on her face. She hugged her too and kissed her on the forehead. They loved the affection Achu showed towards them. Achu pulled Deepthi and to sit near her. They chatted about Deepthi – Abhinav's love story and girlish conversations.

Abhinav talked to them for some time. He went to his room, followed by Wolfie. Wolfie pulled its blanket from the corner of the bed and lay comfortably. Abhinav laid next to Wolfie and patted it softly. Wolfie loved it and slowly it went to sleep. Next to him Abhinav went to sleep soon putting his arm around him.

Deepthi went to the kitchen to help Abhinav's mother preparing the steamed rice with mutton gravy and chicken chukka. Abhinav loved it all the time. No one can know more about a person than their mom. Mom is the only soul who never takes rest whether her child is happy or gloomy. Opening the door silently, Achu crawled into Abhinav's room. Wolfie raised his head slightly to see who's getting in and again lowered. Achu made her steps so cautious. She came to the other end of the bed, taking her mobile phone out. She rubbed on the forehead of Wolfie. He again raised his head and saw her.

"Say Cheeseee...." She said to him and took a selfie with him, while Abhinav was still asleep tightly hugging Wolfie.

'With the Devadoss and his very own companion of all time,' Achu uploaded the pic in Instagram and Facebook in no seconds with the above caption. Wolfie looked so innocently towards the camera, while she took the picture, funny.

Achu had a bath and jumped into white half sleeve top and embroidery pant. She came to the living room, positioned the table fan towards her hair to dry.

"Uncle, did you investigate them correctly? I suspect Abhinav. He might have convinced Deepthi for marriage before and then brought her here. You can believe your kid, but I can't believe these generation kids above the age of three," She giggled.

"Whatever, my son's happiness is my pleasure. And even for our life time boon we got Deepthi. One cannot get a girl like her so easily."

"True. I agree to your statement. You are going to have a nice daughter in law, who won't change the channels while you're are watching the serials." Both of them laughed loudly.

She felt someone patting on her shoulder. There stood Abhinav with a jug of water. Without giving time to react, he poured everything all over her head. Achu faked crying, sat as she was before. Abhinav came in front of her and mocked.

"For the amazing pic you posted."

"Going to kill you idiot..." Achu screamed and plucked his hair with both hands.

03 – Sep – 2016

Sumi kicked the blanket and sat on the bed. She stretched her body and her arms. She gave a yawn and got up from the bed, tied her hair and switched into the denim shorts and a pink sleeveless. It was 9 am. Admiring the nature's beauty by the view from the window, she prepared the tea in the kitchen. Their newly bought Villa had a great view of the Neelankarai Beach. The deep blue sea reflected the rays of the Sun with golden shattered glitters.

Inhaling the aroma of the tea, she poured it in two mugs. She took that in her both hands and went into the bedroom. She searched for John. He was not there. She kept the mug on the tea table at the left side of the bed. Seated on the bed, she kept a pillow near the abdomen. Thinking about John and his love towards her she felt the feel of his manliness. Being handsome won't makes a man, until his care resembles him towards his girl. She knew no man in this planet could love her more than John,

She pulled the curtains of the window down and let the rays of Sun comes into the room. She rolled the blanket and put it at the side of the bed. John came from the bathroom after a fresh bath. He dried his head with a towel. Sumi smiled and came towards him. Hugged him and gave a peck on his cheek.

"Wait for me, I'll freshen up and come," She whispered seductively.

He giggled and kissed her forehead. She hugged him again and melted in his warmth.

He chose a Purple & black lined formal shirt and light cream coloured cotton pant for the day. He stood in front of the mirror and looked his personality with that new shirt. Sumi wasn't ready. He sat at the arm chair and made a phone call.

"Is everything ready?" John asked the guy on the other side of the receiver.

"Almost Sir, you can come with madam She will love it so much."

"Thanks Mr. Hasan."

"Our pleasure Sir," Hasan replied.

John took the balance cup of tea and took a sip. He remembered all the golden days he had and was having with Sumi. She came like a storm in his life and was glooming as a flower day by day. John had another sip and noticed how she treated him every time. She saw him like a kid and pampered him every time. She knew about his past life. But who cares, that was her mind. She loved him a lot and her love never reduced. Opposite to that, it increased every sixty seconds.

Love is not a lifetime agreement. It is the agreement of two souls, which leads to a good life. Marriage is a small announcement to the society where we live. It is just a function to show them, 'Yes we are married and we can have a good life in future and we can make love without any hesitation.' That's how marriages happen in our society.

Sumi and John were not that type. And they knew what they deserved. They knew well about each other and loved each other. No one could complete them than each other. They weren't married in front of the society. But they were happily married with their souls and tied a knot long before.

Relationship needs trust and love. Small … small… fights are welcomed always. And it will end every time with a sorry glance or a tight hug.

Sumi stirred the water with her legs. She felt the sensations of the chillness in the water. Also she sensed the bubbles fizzing around her toes. She rested her back on the tub and took the hand shower and started bathing. She added some rose scented bath salts and rested her hands on the tub, putting her back lowered inside the tub. She closed her eyes, inhaling the fragrance. She touched her hair and her ears like John did last evening. She giggled thinking of her wildness. She felt shy thinking about it again and again.

The fragrance of the bath salts mixed well with the water. She felt her feminine aroma combined with that rose scent. She showered for half an hour and then dried her up with the towel and tied the towel above her breasts covering her body till her thighs. She sat on the dressing table and dried her hair with the hair dryer. John got up and walked towards her. Her heart skipped a beat for his every few footstep. He put his hands on her shoulders firmly, looking in the mirror,

"You looks so stunning baby. Like the pleasant falls in the Amboli, Goa."

Ignoring his praise, Sumi interrogated him with childishness.

"Honey, you haven't taken me there, last time. No issues. Take me there, next month."

"So you didn't care my praise? You funny sweetie," He laughed.

She smiled of her madness. She slipped from the towel and changed into a black full length party gown. She looked herself in mirror and combed her hair. John took that and put a pony of it. He kissed her on the forehead. When his bottom lip released its touch from softness of her skin, she gave a happy smile and a hug.

John opened the car door and Sumi sat inside comfortably. She was cautious that no sprinkles ruined her fantastic black gown. John put the seat belt around her and tightened it. They exchanged their smile.

Sumi's phone buzzed. She took and read her whatsapp message. It was from Deepthi.

"Hey hi love birdies, we have confirmed the date for our marriage. It's on December 3rd. You are the bride's maid and John should be the groom's mate. Wanted to share it with you face to face. But we fixed it suddenly and Achu is here too. I am going to get married baby. Love you so much."

Sumi howled in joy as she read the message completely. She showed it to John too. He called Abhinav and wished him & Deepthi.

Sumi dropped a tear of mere happiness. Blissful moments are very rare and they have at last found themselves together.

Surprise Temptations

To the man of my smile and blush,

You came near me, and played with my dreams. My instinct was really cautious, but he lured inside me what he needed. Keeping me in side his heart, he melted from my forehead up to my toe. I donno whether he is coated on me or not. But I know for sure, he is the coat I love to be on me. He made me feel like the only precious flower of this planet. Kurinji blooms once in 12 years, but girls are those flowers that blooms every day. He used to say my lips resembles strawberries. Whatever, I just want to be his. I know I am the love of his life. He was patient even when my father slapped him. He did everything what a man should do for a girl as a dad, friend and a husband. What should I call him? As I always call, Gentleman? No, you are the pakka gentleman I ever seen. But you deserve more.

So, how can I call him in future? Purusha, Kanava, Anba, Kadhala?? Ok, I am fine with 'Purusha' and 'Anba'. But how will he call me in future? Manaivi, Pondatti, Kadhali?

Purusha, I want to be summoned by 'Ratchasi' from you da. Call me once. I'll be the one who happily close my eyes with all your love with me inside the wooden or steel box. Who cares that. I want to live heartily with you. For 100 years my darling.

your Ravishing Bae.

'Saved in Drafts' pop up shown in her mailbox. She stood up and placed her laptop on the bed.

"Still three months to go. To lighten your house... Sorry!! Our house. :-p " Sent to Abhinav. "Come and lighten now itself," He replied back.

"Matchbox please," She sent and giggled mischievously.

"Go left, the kitchen is there," The reply came.

'Love you to the core,' He passed that in the air. 'What a girl can do when she has the bliss enormously!!!! ' She blushed as she turned pink.

The easiest way to receive one's love is to give love. You can shower love on anyone or anything. Of course, you can love a stranger. Of course it's possible to love a human being if you don't know them too well. But you can never leave when you love them. Love is not just a word, it's an emotion. The simple and strongest emotion which stables this planet still and forever.

John came towards the left door of the car and opened it. Sumi stepped out from the vehicle holding a corner of her pretty black gown in one hand. Mr. Hasan came forward and invited both.

"Did you arrange for any massive proposal today?" She asked John.

He walked past the entrance with her calmly to the hall. John was so obsessed with the love on her and he never missed a chance to make her feel happy. Moreover, that it was his happiness which resided in her.

A red carpet was put nicely on the grey marble floor. Sumi stunned the eyes of the people present in the hall. Dazzling like Emma Watson, she walked on the red carpet with pure elegance and a pretty ramp style. Within a few steps distance to the hall, she saw John standing behind of her. She tilted her head and gave a gaze to hold her hands. He stood smiling there, leaving her puzzled.

A loud voice came from the speaker. "Let's Welcome, Ms. Sumi. She is the reason for these wonderful collection of clicks of this evening." Mr. Hasan gave an intro about Sumi to the audience.

The screens were pulled aside and the photographs of Sumi were decorated all over the walls of the halls. She stood speechless in the mid of the hall, in that pretty black gown with her eyes of joy.

Mr. Hasan delivered a cheque of twenty lakhs Indian rupees to Sumi for her thirty pictures. "Mr. John talked with the interested people for the bids and arranged for this exhibition madam," He said.

Few steps behind her, John stood calm, smiling, and gave a love sigh towards her. She walked towards him and hugged him as the snaps were taken, she gave a cute and sweet mini kiss on his cheek.

Love comes with this choose tag always: *I didn't choose you. You know it is what my heart did.*

12-Oct-2016

Abhinav was busy with his new project and his teammates. He Ignored the call for the sixteenth time. It had been a week since the threat calls started. Deepthi hadn't visited her hometown for a month and more.

Deepthi found Abhinav was worried with these stuffs of the concern towards her. Whenever she talked with her mom, she asked for all these. But what her mom and relatives did was totally ignoring the statement what she asked for.

Love is like a war. It is so easy to begin, but impossible to stop. When it comes to stop, there is the end of your life.

Soon, Deepthi's mom came to the hostel and stayed with her for two days. She tried her utmost to inject the poisonous thoughts of being in the same caste ever and how pure the caste is for the relatives and the strength and all.

Deepthi didn't gave an ear to that. She was simply doing what she wanted. Her mom even begged her in front of her fellow roommates. She remained silent.

Pure love won't just give happiness, it also shows us how we should be rigid and strong until it gets succeed.

When two souls are in love, nothing can tear them apart, than their own hearts.

When I saw you for the first time,

I was afraid to talk with you,

When I talked to you for the first time,

I was afraid to like you,

When I liked you for the first time,

I was afraid to love you,

*Now that **I love you from my soul**,*

I swear to the whole world,

I won't lose you.

Deepthi and Abhinava was so straight in what they wanted. They didn't want to be the flexible ones who go with their parent's decision and marry other person, living a fake masked life until death. They both deserved each other and desire of each other.

Nothing could separate them, until the lovers wanted to get separated. Lovers can lose all battes but love never loses; it wins every battle.

Abhinav designed the invitation cards for them in a WhatsApp styled one. Deepthi liked it too and Achu made some changes in it. Due to the threats from south side, they all planned to do the marriage in Chennai. John booked the 'Shanaya Party hall' for the reception and 'Megha Marriage hall' for the marriage. Sumi opted Thailand for the honeymoon and she booked the tickets for the upcoming marriage couple.

You won't be alone or sad when your friends are with you forever, even when you are in the state of dying. They'll make you happy, keep you joyful with the tears behind that joy. That kind of friends are rare to see. John – Sumi – Deepthi – Abhinav made themselves as that.

19-Oct-2016

"You can get any other girl for your salary and for your skin. Leave my daughter and leave my dignity." Deepthi's father requested Abhinav. They were at the IT Park Food Court.

"Sir, think outside the boundary of the caste system. We both love each other and can't imagine a life with other one. I am eligible for all the terms as a man, human, good mannered and your daughter's lovable man. But still you are sticking with your caste and your unwanted dignity. Think like human Sir, not a caste oriented person."

"So, this is what you say when we come down and talk nicely with you right. Yes, we are believers of the caste system and we won't think more than that. We live in a society of our caste people with the population of 40000 in our town. You won't know how much my family would be degraded if I give my daughter's hand in marriage to a groom from any other caste."

"See dear Sir, I don't know about my caste and all until the joining of my college. During that damn formalities I was supposed to get the community certificate for joining college. That's how I just know about my caste name. And I feel shame to talk about caste and all. In fact, I love to be a kind and broadminded person."

Before he finished, Deepthi's father threw his coffee mug at the wall and walked outside. Everyone in that square place looked on Abhinav. He hadn't changed his look and still sipping the coffee thinking about the plague of this country.

28-Oct-2016

Again Deepthi got the call from her hometown. This time her dad's friend and their community legal advisor Mahendran called her. He tried to tell her how she would live in their home happily if she married his son. Even if she didn't want him he said he will look for another guy of her taste. But all his constraint was inside our caste.

Deepthi was so depressed and tired of answering and responding to them all. She wished if December could come soon.

Behind her tears and her heart, she always hided her hurt feelings and pain. Whenever she saw Abhinav, all she gave was her ultimate care and her lovely smile which always made him to feel better from all the hurt he suffered too.

All she saw was him every day, but she didn't know how to tell him how much he was hers to herself, He was her light when days were dark, she really loved that ... Her man was her angel...

Save the date, It's ours

Deepthi, Sumi, Achu were at 'The Chennai Silks' along with Abhinav and John for the marriage time costume purchases. John opted for sherwani for the reception evening for Abhinav and blazer for himself. Sumi opted choli for her. Achu preferred saree with Deepthi.

They three left Abhinav and Deepthi to choose for their evening and left to select the costumes for them.

"Just 16 days more. You are gonna be mine," Abhinav whispered in her ears.

"Shhhh... We are gonna be ours. Change it," She smiled back.

"Oh Ok. But we are already ours na …" He pulled her leg.

"Yep. You know, still you never felt the softness of my cheeks. Gentleman. Don't worry, am all yours soon as you said."

"Close your eyes Deepthi..." She just stood there closing her eyes and questioning in her mind, what was he going to do.

He took held her hands and came closer. "See the darkness, this is my life without you." Abhinav said innocently.

Even it was an old epic sentence of love, Deepthi loved hearing from him. She knew how sweet he was and how cute his heart was.

A real woman never sees the Guy's wealth and richness. All she care is how he will treat her and how his care will melt her all over the life. She cares about nothing else. In her dream he will be hers. But in his life she is the dream.

Deepthi took a look at the pile of saree which was on the desk. Abhinav sat calmly near her, letting her to choose what she liked. She picked a light green shiny silk saree and showed it to Abhinav. It was well woven by the hands, having a neat border of mountain designing with the silk lining. In the middle of the saree, a couple getting married image was woven neatly. Looked like Radha and Krishna.

In fact, Abhinav was an atheist, but he hadn't seen this as a religious symbol. Broadminded atheists know how to differentiate arts and religions.

"It would be so pretty on you Deepthi. Red colored blouse would be a great match for this," Abhinav took the saree and sent it to the billing section.

Deepthi dragged him to the sherwani section. Abhinav was looking into the collections of the sherwanis. She gave a romantic gaze towards him. He smiled. She smiled. Deepthi took a gray colored, stones covering the shoulder sherwani in one hand and a white colored sherwani in other hand.

Achu ran to them and chose the white one. And she made Abhinav to go for a trail with this.

Deepthi fell on his handsomeness when he arrived with that sherwani on him. He was like Saif Ali khan during his marriage. His lightly trimmed beard, neatly combed hair, straight neck, broad shoulders, in between that a beautiful heart, everything melted her.

Coming closer to her, he was just three steps away. She sensed his perfume very closer. He put his arms around her, pulling her towards him.

There were inches between her cheeks and his lips. He touched her hair and put the front falling strands behind her ear.

"Save the date. It's December 2nd. The day on which we are going to break our first kiss," He told in her ears. She giggled. He smiled naughty. All you need is the comfort with your partner.

07-Nov-2016

John and Abhinav were at Valarsaravakkam police station with Deepthi's father and his friend Mahendran. Heated conversations went between them. Mahendran knew the police officer well. The Sub inspector got his transfer to Valasaravakkam station two years ago by the help of Mahendran using his influence. He also talked in favor of Mahendran.

Mahendran insisted officer to file a case against Abhinav for kidnapping their girl. Deepthi's father was looking furiously towards Abhinav.

"She is safe with my mom and dad. She is willing to be with them in their house. No one can say no to this. Because she is a major and she knows what to do."

John told to all. While talking to Mahendran, Deepthi's father raised his arm and came to beat John. Abhinav blocked and pushed him.

He put the marriage invitation on the table.

"It's not a culture to invite the bride's family for their daughter's marriage. But, what to do. You people are very busy with your caste and your unwanted dignity psycho things. We can deal this case in a fraction of second with John's family lawyer. But the pain you gave to my heart won't erase easily.

Just because of her love on me she suffered much by the family which grew her up. Apart from your daughter's happiness, bliss, joy and all, the shit caste is the only one you care about right. Go with it. If you have some feelings in your heart, you will come for our wedding. Or else I know how to keep my Deepthi happy.

And I will show it in front of your face," Abhinav made her point clear to him and left the place.

Nothing in the world is so bigger than these three - the kindness of the father, the love of the mother, the happiness you see in the face of your loved one.

Officially Yours...

02 – Dec- 2016

Megha Marriage hall was surrounded by happiness that morning. John, Sumi and Achu was busy welcoming their friends and relatives of Abhinav. No one from Deepthi's side attended the wedding.

They completely ignored Deepthi as their girl in their family including her parents. She was complete in sadness even when it was her marriage, only because of her mom and dad's act.

What to do!! The plague of India plays an awesome rule in this Society. When you love a person, you are not allowed to marry. Because that's how we are grown and living, so you have to be like us. That's what the answer will come from the elders.

Sumi wore a peach colored wide gown which had a lovely circle like clouds below her hip. John chose white shirt and blue jeans for the function. After all it was his soul friend's marriage. They both were as happy as they were during their marriage. Teasing your friends when they are getting married is the fun that no friends should miss.

John bit Sumi's ear softly. She gave an angry look and suddenly she melted into laugh.

"Save it for the upcoming days, not today. Be present with the wedding ceremony mentally and physically," She giggled.

Achu was at the entrance welcoming all the people coming to the marriage hall. She sprayed rosewater on them, to feel them refreshed and fragrant. Elegant decoration made the ceremony stand royal. Happiness bloomed all over the place. The day came. They had waited for it so long. Behind this joy and happiness, their untold tears and pain was unwritten.

When a couple are engaged in an arranged marriage, it's like a contract signing. Like they are agreed on the 10th minute of their meet and they are gonna live with each other for 60-70 long years. And the funny thing is, between the time of contract signing on engagement, by numerous calls and texts, the love will be lured. Oh. my fault, they are induced love on each other.

I can't stop laughing when people say arranged ones are so good than love marriages. Yep, I agree they are, in financial and parents support side. Without happiness and our loved ones lap sleep, money is just a pile of ashes.

Silk dhoti and white shirt matched well for Abhinav. With a trimmed beard and moustache, he looked handsome with a well-groomed haircut. Marriage kit facial added some more manliness on his face. And his ever glooming smile made the day pleasant.

John presented a gold ring and chain for Abhinav. He insisted him to wear that and he did. Abhinav hugged John and they both shook their hands.

Guests cheered towards Abhinav and pinched his cheeks for his shyness on his marriage day. He crossed the hall, silently like a cat he went backstage,

'Bride's Room', the letters on the plate was hanging at the top of the wall. Abhinav opened it lightly and peeped in. Deepthi was sitting in front of the dressing table looking herself in the mirror, applying kajal on the bottom of her eyes. Sumi was busy doing flower decorations on her hair.

Abhinav patted softly on Sumi's shoulder. With a slight fear she turned and looked him. She giggled and silently went outside leaving love birds alone. Deepthi didn't felt the presence of Abhinav, as she was busy applying kajal on her eyes.

He stood near the door, admiring the beauty of Deepthi. It's very true that girls become so beautiful on their marriage day not only because of makeup, but the thing is that's their special day to step up in the new life. The bliss of marriage, the joy to hold their man's hand and show the world that am getting married.... how sweet was that for girl. She will feel complete when her man would tie the knot with her.

Deepthi wore full length bindi colored saree which touched her feet with the floor. The saree was woven with the ethnic style of Kanchipuram style silk material. On the borders, the pictures of Tanjore Big Temple, Nellaiappar Temple, Pamban Bridge, Kodaikanal Western Ghats, Madurai Meenakshi Temple was woven too.

She looked so fresh and curious towards her marriage. She knew how Abhinav loves her soul. She always waited for this. To give herself beautifully in his hands was the one she desired of.

Living a life unwillingly, for the sake of parents arranged in order make them happy, is the most coward thing you could do for the girl who enters her marriage life with you.

Abhinav looked on the mirror, which reflected the curvy neck of her shining with the green stone necklace. She was applying the mid line of the kajal. Abhinav went towards her, walking slowly. She felt his presence, as she noticed him via mirror. She smiled with the blossom round face which made Abhinav fall towards her. The halfmoon forehead of hers had a small mark of bindi.

Jhumki earrings of her jumped whenever she giggled. She applied a very less makeup of her cheeks and chin. Women are so beautiful with their eyes. Blue colored eyeshadow looked adorable on her. With the lovely soft peach cheek she attracted Abhinav' eyes on it. She turned red and her cheeks got super blushed.

He touched her right cheek and rubbed it softly as she loved it at this special time. He caressed it slowly and felt the softness of it as she looked into his eyes, saying about her feelings, without uttering a single word by mouth.

She hugged him putting her hands around his waist and laying her head on his belly. Gazing into her eyes, he rose her chin and looked on her lips.

Her lovely full lips was coated with strawberry colored lipstick. She cared so good with the coating during the time she applied.

"Finally my man came to taste my lipstick" said Deepthi showing her eagerness towards him.

He raised his right eyebrow and teased her with a wink and a smile.

"There is no replacement for the taste of raw lips, Honey," He replied.

She took a tissue and slowly removed her lipstick coating. Even when she removed it, her full lips were rosy glossy, looking like the ripe strawberries. Abhinav came closer, holding her hands. He took it to his shoulder and placed it.

"As I promised to our love, I am giving myself pure and truly." He said with his honesty.

Does a girl need any other than this from a guy? Definitely not!!

Deepthi rested her head on his other shoulder and shed her tears with a blissful soul. You mustn't understand how much it means, when you marry your loved one, after a long war and entering into the marriage life with her/him until you fall in love like that.

Abhinav was seated in the marriage stage as the groom and spelling the mantras with the priest. He had no interest in having the mantras and all, but his mother insisted him to be like a normal guy for that day at least. Atheists are always treated as aliens.

Sumi took Deepthi to the marriage hall. Deepthi looked so beautiful and pure like a swan. With tiny steps slowly, she came to the marriage stage. As she was few steps behind the stage, suddenly the speakers started singing.

'Thudakkam Mangalyam' song from Bangalore days played in the background. Within a few seconds, Abhinav jumped from the stage to the ramp and a small crew was behind and danced with him. John joined with Abhinav and winked Sumi. She too came and joined with them.

Amidst of the dance, in the mid of all, Abhinav took the mic in hands. With the loud breathing, "I just can't wait to marry the love of my life, you Deepthi. Love you Chello..!! "

He came to the stage back and sat with Deepthi. They both shared the mantras with the priest.

"If my love for you apart from the caste is a crime, I want to be the most wanted criminal of this India to have you in my life baby." Deepthi told as she held his fingers firmly while saying mantras.

"Ketti melam... Ketti melam…" The priest signaled all. The drums and instruments of the Tamil wedding style Ketti Melam showered the marriage blessings all over the hall.

In the middle of that, John brought a big collage of Sarah, with her lovely pics with Abhinav and his family. It brought their tears, but somehow they managed to be the joy of Abhinav getting married while she was watching.

Abhinav took the mangalsutra from the priest's hand, as Deepthi came near her bending her neck to make his comfortable. He tied the three knots of mangalsutra on her neck.

Moments after that, 'Metti' wearing event was started. Abhinav was in his knees and Deepthi's right leg palm was on his hands. He starred at her fingers. With the nice coat of Mehandi with her lemonish skin, it attracted him in front of all.

He touched it softly all she felt his care and smiled back with shyness. She knew how he would treat her. She would be the princess of their own world.

If he wants you ever to be in his life all the time, you don't have to fight for that place ever, he 'll simply keep you there at the high and make you smile all the time.

When you want your partner to feel special, the sweetest thing you can do is, letting her know that she's / he's always in your heart and in your soul in every moment of your life.

'Metti' is a small silver ornament, should be wore on the index finger by the groom, after the groom ties mangalsutra on the bride. It's a traditional function getting followed for years.

Abhinav's mom brought the metti and gave it in his hands. He shifted her palm to his left hand and had the metti on his right.

"The day I will be on knees for another one girl, it will be the day in which I tie a shoe lace for our daughter."

Deepthi looked into his eyes. In a no time, she bent herself and kissed his forehead, hugging him partially. Abhinav slowly put the metti on her finger.

John told in air "Ours is upcoming. Be ready" to the love of his life. Sumi turned red in blush as she heard this.

In the mid of my dream, I desired to go with it

I knew it was a dream, But I never wanted to leave from it

I saw her eyes, Looking for me

No match found still, when her eyes met me sharp

Eye to eye, Melted in her gaze

Dissolved myself in her looks, Cherished with her love

She ate me with that, I started to love it inch by inch

The magical moment, The very necessary moment of every guy's life

I admit we weren't just lovers, I admit we weren't just friends

She grabbed my hands, Pulled me towards her

Come and see the beauty of Pattaya,sShe whisphered

With mere happiness, I was out of words.

I wanted to say something, But I couldn't

I can't never see such beauty in my life, I said pointing her

I know I blurted it out, but that wasn't the first time

She looked, Tilting her head slightly

She pulled me again, Keeping her face on my chest

Rubbed her hands on my cheeks, pinched it softly

Her words are so true, it is our bonding

"I am your better half and I will be with you forever."

You are my everything!

It was a casual weekend. Deepthi came from the pooja room finishing the daily pooja for her desired gods. Abhinav was in sound sleep. It was seven in the morning. They were married for two months. Since, caste played a volleyball in their life, they overcame it all with their strong love, determination and the trust they have on each other.

Abhinav and Deepthi moved to their new apartment at Besant Nagar. As a gift for his marriage John gifted him this. But he cordially denied it and asked for him to arrange a housing loan for him as a gift. John nodded for that and he did it.

Deepthi requested Abhinav's mom and dad to come to stay with us for plenty of times. They denied it softly, because they wanted to live in their town until they die. So, after that Deepthi and Abhinav hadn't compelled them. They planned to visit them between every odd weekends.

When the alarm rings at nine, Abhinav woke up. He pulled his trousers down and put a pair of tracks and sleeveless shirt. With a light trimmed beard, he looked handsome even she didn't take his bath at morning. Deepthi placed coffee on the dressing table minutes before. He took a sip and smiled to himself.

Now-a-days, it's very hard to get a girl who makes a bed coffee for you. Somewhere he saw in meme that ' Marry a girl who makes bed coffee for you. She is precious.' It crossed his mind and he smiled again taking a sip of coffee.

He heard Deepthi was making pooris for the breakfast. Entering the kitchen, he took a knife with some onions. They both exchanged a glance for few seconds. Abhinav stood opposite to her and started chopping onions for the sabji.

Deepthi turned to the shelf to take the mustard box. Her height was not up to the top of the shelf as she lifted her hand as much she could. Amidst of this, Abhinav noticed her small and tiny raw spicy belly. After a long honeymoon at Thailand, still he felt himself spicy many times. Some said love is for 60 days and lust is for 30 days. But that's not true, if you get your loved partner as your life partner.

She was in an orange T-shirt which had a neat round neck and a long white skirt. He couldn't resist more, he simply buried his face on her belly button. She got goose bumps and she shivered with the sudden caress of her hubby. She almost lost the balance and was about to fall. Abhinav made a perfect catch as her lips touched his 0.5mm beards on his cheek. He gave a smile and she smacked light on his head.

They both finished the lunch at 2.30 pm. Deepthi was talking with Sumi during the meantime, while Abhinav had his food slowly tasting every rice with Deepthi's special chicken chettinad gravy. Sumi went to Assam for making a documentary about birds and its preservation in India. She was with her team, exploring the birds and its types of living and all. She said that John was busy with his dad's business. He was yet to come with her, but she denied and told him to carry on the work with his dad.

Deepthi laid on the sofa with her legs crossed. Abhinav finished his lunch and sat on the floor touching his love's palm.

"So, its again a casual weekend with foot relaxation therapy again. Go on" Deepthi put her legs down.

Abhinav took her right leg in his hand and started massaging slowly on the sides of her leg. It was feeling nice and Deepthi loved to have it every week. In fact, if every husband did that to every wife, they'd wait eagerly for that every week.

Amidst of this. He never left the chance of feeling the softness of her palm. He took thumb and massaged it. This went same to the rest. He continued it for the left leg too.

Everyone loved to have that kind of massage during pregnancy. The legs get hurt daily because of the weight increases during that time. Woman like to have the foot relaxation massage after their 5th month every week. But men are very busy with their works and other stuffs. Only a very men care about it seriously.

Deepthi was very happy all the time, because of her sweet and lovable husband. He never gave her a chance to point out him wrong.

Men who are perfect in love, can't be denied.

After some time, he left Deepthi to have a little sleep on the sofa itself. She sensed the aroma of Abhinav's gulab jamun as she woke up at six in the evening. He was preparing it with rose flavoured essence mixed with jeera.

"Hey Kitty, get refreshed and come to have this sweet."

"Awww... Thank you my love. Trust me, your heart and care is lakh times sweeter than your jamuns."

"So, my jamuns are bad!!" He teased her and she loved it. She washed her face and untied her hair.

Like a black desert it covered the sides of her face. Within that dark black forest, her face looked lime in a small sodium bulb light.

They both had the sweet sitting opposite to each other, sharing with the spoons and loads of love. She was amused when she saw the aqua nail polishes on her fingers. She hugged him and kissed his cheek for minutes.

If you want to know true love still exists, be the one and let others to know you as an example.

In the society of male domination and unequal treating of wife, Abhinav stood tall always in Deepthi's heart.

12 – Mar – 2017

To the man of my smile and blush,

I heard stories about seven lives. During my childhood I believed in pre life too. But nowadays, I think I have to believe strongly in that. Because I never seen a lovely man like you in my life. And if the pre life of everyone exists I must had meditated to god for 100 long years to get you in this life. Before our love you ran for me to the pharmacy when I am sick. Now you are spending all your time with me, treating like a princess of our own built kingdom.

Am I the one who is lucky in this world?? Do you know am a simple girl named 'Deepthi' that's it. My heart never accepted the fact that my parents rejected you completely. They are out of their mind. In this four month of our marriage life, I never felt like missing you. Coz, you never gave me a chance to say I don't like this. How can a man be so much adorable?

I heard about the man in Cindrella stories. I see you in the form of that. Girls are not satisfied only for physical pleasure, darling. They last for the care and the kindness shown by their love to them. You are a pro in that, being such innocent. Love me more and more always like. The love you show on me is infinite. Mr. Gentleman.

−   your Ravishing Bae

The duty of a man is to shower all his love on the girl who is the love of his life. Passion, Deliberation, Anxious, Exciting, everything can make a girl's heart more beautiful than anything.

Destiny of Love

14 – April – 2017

Deepthi fell onto the ground and fainted. Her office manager called the ambulance and sent two of her colleagues with her to the hospital. Doctor asked Deepthi to call her husband. But she denied. She wanted to tell him by her words.

It was the life of their love. Deepthi was seven weeks pregnant. Her colleagues Anitha and Ranjana congratulated her. They forced her to convey the happy news to her husband.

Deepthi wanted to make it special. Every girl dream is to feel her child inside her.

There is no better feeling in this world than the movement of their life inside them.

Anitha and Ranjana bought laddu for the whole office and distributed it to everyone. Deepthi was blushing every second. She touched her belly softly.

"I don't know who you'll be, but I know you are our everything," Deepthi told to her child inside.

Abhinav came home earlier than her that evening. He was reading the 'All Rights Reserved for You'. Deepthi entered the house with her usual pretty smile on her face.

"Hey, came so early ??"

"Yes, sweetheart. Work was not much today. Felt little bit tired. So, came early."

"Seems you are so happy today. Any reason?" he added.

She tried to hide her blush almost. But it came little bit out of control. Somehow she managed.

"Nothing dear, Ranjana's sissy got pregnant. So we went to her home and was with her for some time."

"Great. She has to be cherished with a wide amount of happiness"

"True. She loves to have her hubby hugging her all the time," Deepthi giggled.

"As you promised, this Sunday you have to take me for the Hanuman Temple. Keep that in mind, you made a promise," She added.

"Mmm. Ok. But like every time I'll stay outside until you worship and come."

"You can't be changed."

"I never want to," He laughed.

17 – April – 2017

"Pick that blue one. I must need it soon."

She said curiously with her hands pointing that in the air.

"Just a single one?? I'll grab a bunch of them," Abhinav replied her.

"You are so sweet."

She tried to reach his head to hold. He just went near her. She couldn't get up and sat again repeatedly, so he leaned towards her.

Deepthi touched his head fondly.

"You are my heaven," She smiled and expressed. Abhinav was in love with her lips which gave a wonderful smile of her.

"Am lucky to be a family with you and this buddy inside you." He touched her belly softly. Got the bill and put the blue packed child diapers of six numbers inside the bag and started walking with her.

Abhinav got up from his dream, while Deepthi remembered his promise once again. He got goose bumps by that dream and he explained it to her. Deepthi was pro in hiding the feelings, she simply admired the way he told to her and expressions he gave.

She wore a pink designer silk saree and had jasmine flowers on her hair. She opened the almirah and brought the yellow shirt and dhoti for Abhinav. After taking the bath, Abhinav was in the clothes she chose for him. He folded the sleeves for some inches. He groomed himself as Deepthi sat on the sofa with her lap playing music.

To the man of my smile and blush,

I can't wait sweetheart, but my whole mind says me to remain with the silence up to some time. I know you are allergic to temples and gods, as you say always, it is a place where only painful and thanks giving souls resides daily. But I desire to be a thanks giving one today, you should have fished something special seeing my blushes and happiness on my face. Then why didn't you??

You are so sweet my innocent, baby, you are in enormous love with me. Still you haven't asked me what's the reason, what's special and all. Did I make any long years' prayers to get you? Or it was just meant us to be together? And I am smiling happily day by day by your true and purest love. You are the best thing happened in my life.

The very special thing is another one upcoming. We are going to be there. I want to open this to you soon today and deliberately want to see your expression at that time. Seriously, I don't know whether I'll get butterflies inside my stomach or whether I'll get shivers through my spine when I say this to you.

One thing I can say.... you are the meaning of all this came to me. I love you. I love you more and more every second of our life. You complete me and our little upcoming baby is going to complete us.

Wait... Still I want to say you something.

*If it's a girl baby, I want to name her as **Sarah** .*

Always with love,

−   your Ravishing Bae

Deepthi kept the lap aside as she typed all that for her love. She wanted to disclose this and all her writings, desire and the expressive untold letters to Abhinav on that day itself.

Abhinav was ready and was about to kick-start the bike. Deepthi locked the door and sat behind him, putting her arm on his shoulder. She went near his ear and bit it softly. He loved of the sensation given by his wife.

They were heading to the temple.

Deepthi thought of revealing about her pregnancy to him at the temple. But what if he'll scream due to the happiness.

"Baby, after temple. Can we go for Ibaco?"

"Seri chellam, we'll go," he replied. She smiled and her fingers ran through his hair.

They crossed the Alandur metro and on the way near Aasife hotel on G.S.T road.

Deepthi heard some noise and turned back. Just then she saw a big stone came in a huge force and was about to hit Abhinav's on his shoulder. He lost the balance and they both fell on the ground. The bike went aside, getting its tires screeching.

Abhinav was about to get up and gave a hand for Deepthi. A long galvanized pipe hit on his spine. Deepthi screamed loudly, seeing Abhinav getting hit with that long pipe. He fell on the ground with pain. Deepthi recognized the faces. They were totally seven.

They were her cousin brothers and two of them were so close with their community operations.

Deepthi asked for help to people there. Everyone was in fear to do. What a poor girl can do at that time, she can scream or cry with the pain. Abhinav got up and ran towards Deepthi to make her safe. One of the guy in that gang, caught him and other one hit his thigh with the pipe.

Abhinav was on his knees trying to reach out Deepthi. In a no time, three of them started giving fist punches to Abhinav. He was in bloodshed and was about to faint.

"Leave him. Leave us alone. Am pregnant. We need to live our life. We won't come in your eyes ever again," She pleaded them.

Deepthi tried to push every one of them who were assaulting Abhinav. His eyes were on Deepthi, staring at her pleading towards them. His heart felt joy as he heard his love was pregnant. But how could a guy feel that happiness in a bad state like this.

Siva, her elder cousin brother pushed her aside and made a deep cut on Abhinav's hand with the knife. Deepthi was shocked and sat on the ground crying heavily. Aadhi, the next cousin brother of her came and slapped her in the face.

They were heavily intoxicated with the casteism, which ruined their humanity inside. Moreover than that, they were heavily mastered to sweep the kindness out and filling the caste blood inside.

Deepthi pushed Aadhi and ran towards Abhinav. Her hands touched the ground as she felt another hard slap on her face by Siva. He had her hair in his hand and dragged her near Abhinav. Her pain, her screams, her tears, nothing stopped their cruelty.

In the eye sight of Abhinav, he took the knife and made a deep slit on her throat. She was dead in less than thirty seconds as her body left with no motion in it.

Abhinav cried like being in hell. It was like killing him lakhs and lakhs of time, tearing his skin apart and slicing him alive. He tried to reach her hands, but he couldn't. In the next few seconds, he was torn by several knives and sickles.

After twenty minutes of that gang left the place, police came and gave a report of the murder. Deepthi's eyes was staring towards Abhinav in bloodshed. Abhinav's body was left with twenty-six deep cuts on him.

Epilogue

After the death of Abhinav and Deepthi, John went furious towards the killers. But his dad made him calm and filed a case against Deepthi's cousins and her dad. Sumi was in a coffee shop at Anna Salai. A politician who was the leader of a specific caste spoke.

"If guys from other caste looks for our girl to marry, I swear to god that I'll kill him and his entire group in their mom's womb itself. Let's take a pledge to do it," He shouted. And the crowd responded "Yes..."

Sumi went from the coffee shop, without having anything with tears on her eyes. Sumi went to her hometown for some days to get consoled by her family for having lost her best friend.

Assistant Commissioner Vikram was appointed to investigate this case on high priority. Tamil Nadu was shaken by this cruel murders of a love couple by their own family.

India is a democratic and secular country, but still when a hero rises to the top, when a politician addresses him, people are so fond to know about his religion and caste. They take it as a matter of pride and honour.

When a girl of our country won the Silver Medal in badminton, the number of google searches about her is very less than the number of google searches about 'Which caste she was?' Still we are adjusting and get adjusted with the society we are living in.

Love marriages are looked like a sin by our society. The society is us, we are the people who comprise the society and we are the people still live with the stains of the society.

Social Reputation, Social Stigma, Social Approval, these three factors are the things which plays in your life whether your parents agree for your love marriage or not.

According to Indian parents, you should never talk with the stranger. But after the 10 minutes of Groom's visit to Bride's home for just a casual meet after matrimonial match, you can talk with him.

Even one of my friend's friend never seen her groom before the marriage. She saw him just 10 – 15 minutes before the marriage. Being obedient in certain things are respectful, but being okay for every decision of parents will make you being a slave.

You people can ask 'What if love marriages are made compulsory in India? At least after that it can be reduced right!!?' Never. If love marriages are compulsory in India, the parents will look for a groom & bride and will make them fall in love with each other.

Deepthi said that she loved Abhinav to the society she lived. But what the society said was that she couldn't marry him, because she loved him. It is the fact happening all over India for years and decades.

Casteism is the plague of our country. It plays a vital role in politics, business, family etc., People love to put their caste name behind their real names. They think it's a matter of pride. Is it? Is that a pride thing to do?

Humanity is the pride thing buddy. Helping, showing kindness, showering care that makes you human. Live a life like that and generations will talk about your pride and honour.

According to some reports, nearly 250 honour killings are happening in India every year. The people who choose their life partners are getting killed. You can share your bed and yourself with the guy/girl whom your parents choose. But, you can never think about a life with your loved one in this casteism filled jumbo society.

Be human. Have humanity. Save generations.